To LIV,

Thanks for bringing your
fire to a very cold Liverpool.

Yours,
C

look and Despair

Music is the master key to the stories around me.
Feel free to jump with me into the End's soundtrack.

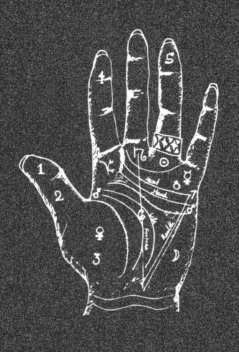

Llegarás mañana
Para el fin del mundo
O el año nuevo
El puerto se llena
De barcos de guerra
Y una lluvia fina
De cenizas cae
Salgo a encontrarte en mi traje
Mi traje de tierra

-'*Para el Fin del Mundo o el Año Nuevo*',
Lhasa de Sela

I vow to thee, my country, all earthly things above,
Entire and whole and perfect, the service of my love;
The love that asks no questions, the love that stands the test,
That lays upon the altar the dearest and the best;
The love that never falters, the love that pays the price,
The love that makes undaunted the final sacrifice.

-'*I vow to thee, my country*',
Sir Cecil Spring Rice
to the tune of 'Jupiter',
by Holst

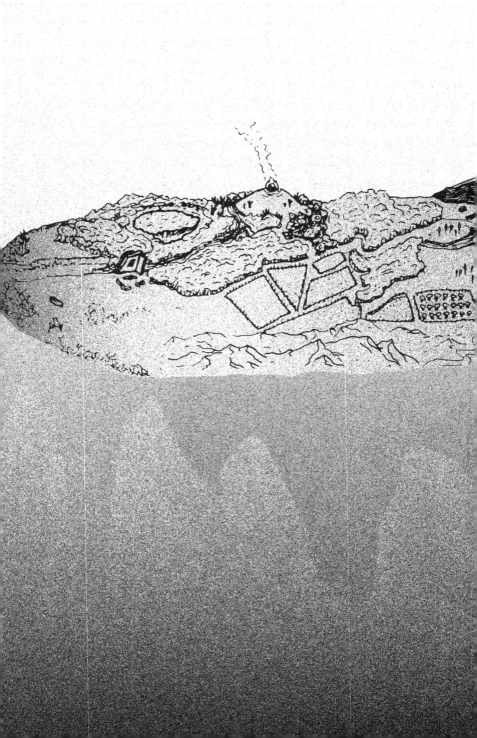

I - THE SUN

In which a dog is hungry; a boy knits; a mother sleeps; and Lázaro sees his father.

'We haven't heard news from any village around Ronda in weeks,' Lázaro lamented.

The truth is that the boy couldn't tell wether it had been weeks, days or seconds. For in that cursed village the Sun never set, but remained permanently in the sky; forever on the verge of setting, never providing the star-studded gift of night.

Lázaro observed the bright orange sunset from the top of the city's dangerous cliff. Behind him, the small village of Ronda crowned the capricious rock formations, a white bird nesting on top of a sleeping golem. Those who lived in Ronda shouldn't fear the heights. In front of him and after the imminent drop, miles of green and yellow fields, perfectly delimited by the callous hands of the families who made a living out of them. They worked these fields in exchange for very little money, just so nobility could eat. Lázaro closed his eyes, he could almost smell the spilt sweat and blood transforming the barren land into a fertile, olive oil-scented dream in front of him. The whole region was graced by the eerie orange sunlight, and the bodies of the villagers could not escape the eternal glow clashing against their skin. The beams danced around the adorning gargoyles and lemon trees, leaving no corner untouched. The Great Bridge of Ronda, linking the two sides of a huge canyon that split the city in half, merged the Old and New parts of the settlement in ways more than just the literal. In a city divided by a chasm, whoever held the bridge held the power. The man-made structure rose over the eroding river, and stood there proud, clearly visible to the arriving wanderers.

'Night would be a relief for once,' Lázaro sighed, tired. Even the clouds in the sky had remained the same all along. He knew every single one of them by now. The boot-shaped cloud to the North by the New City of Ronda, the sparrow-shaped one right above them in the Old City, the three little ones moving towards the horizon, and then the cross-shaped one that graced the sky like an earring made out of rose coral. Not a drop of wind helped the clouds travel, for Ronda was cursed.

Time had died.

The young boy turned around and started to walk towards his house. The Sun never finished its journey behind the horizon, but every once in a while, Lázaro enjoyed lying in his bed pretending that his body needed sleep. *It is boring, but what isn't these days? It would also be nice to check up on mum.* He comforted himself, as he tried to break the forced routine in which he was trapped. Sometimes he would walk aimlessly around town, but those walks would always lead him to one of the gardens that hung on the edges of the cliff. Once there, he would think about everything and anything, although there were a couple of questions that assaulted him regularly.

Is it something inside my head that stopped working, and I can't tell minutes from days? Or perhaps, days had always been like this? Mornings, nights and middays may have been just an annoying dream - or maybe, yes, time has really left us and I am the only one in the whole damned place who can tell. He never found answers, only more questions. The curse had provided no hints as to its rules, its goal or what actually caused it. It was all up to Lázaro's curious mind.

On his way home, he observed the villagers of Ronda; the elders María, Perpetua and Eustaquia were sitting at the front of their whitewashed houses, just as they usually did during Summer sunsets. The ancient ladies would wash their front door steps at the end of every day. Then they would each take out a handmade bulrush chair, settle into it and chat the Sun away. The water below their feet evaporated slowly, thanks to the heat stored in the stone during such hot days.

'The smell of the Earth,' the ladies whispered to themselves in unison as Lázaro walked past them.

How sad it is that the ladies haven't been inside their houses in ages, only there, by their front steps. I wish they would stop waiting for a night that will never arrive. The boy exercised compassion, as he tried to contain a scream that said *Wake up! Time is frozen! There's nothing left to wait for!*

'Look Perpetua, look María. It's the boy of the Mondragón's servants. Lazarillo! Come! Give some conversation to these old women! You never know how long we have left before our Heavenly Lord takes us back to him,' commanded elder Eustaquia.

'That's if he thinks you are a deserving company, Eustaquia. People talk. I'm half deaf and even I've heard enough stories about your behaviour that'd send you straight to Hell, so I'm guessing He has too!' said Perpetua, causing the three to burst into witch-like laughter. Lázaro's skin crawled at the sound of potential witches hiding in plain sight.

'Well, all of those tales took place when I was younger. I'm too old for that kind of mischief now,' murmured Eustaquia haughtily, after catching her breath. The boy, struggling against the scream building up inside of him, didn't stop to entertain the women.

'Sorry ladies, but I'm running some chores for my mother. I'll try and stay with you for a bit later,' said Lázaro, walking as fast as his legs allowed him. The boy was in no mood for

15

meaningless conversations. He wished his legs were longer so he could make a quicker escape. Even after he walked two streets away from them he could still hear them howling. It was as if the three ladies were ecstatic about the whole situation. *After all, they were on the verge of their final days... and look at them now, receiving extra time to gossip all they want. Thanks to the curse!* Reasoned Lázaro, trying to find an answer to everything, as he usually did. But little they knew of the End.

Planted geraniums rejoiced in the cursed light, hanging from bright white walls and sheltered by red roof tiles. Lázaro related to the coloured flowers, they also seemed to have something to say, but no one was listening - they struggled to convey the message as much as the boy. He admired them in their stoic silence, reassuring them that he already knew: The End was coming. The villagers simply chose not to pay attention to the signs, such as their shadows becoming thinner or how their words became increasingly difficult to get out of their throats, as if anchored at the bottom of their chests. The boy walked faster, feeling every single little stone in the pavement through the soles of his worn-out shoes. His friend Pablo's old greyhound stared blankly into the void while a few flies buzzed around, circling the dog's food. The same flies had been there since time had stopped, Lázaro was so used to them that he'd even thought about naming the insects, but he couldn't tell which one was which in their eternal movement. Pablo hadn't been out to play since the curse had started. Lázaro got the same excuse every single time he tried to break the cycle.

'I am helping my mother knit,' Pablo's voice called out from a slightly ajar door.

'Knitting? In this heat? Are you trying to raise bed bugs? Tell your mother it's going to be only for an hour and then you'll be back - please!' begged Lázaro. He did so more passionately every time, but to no avail.

'Sorry Lazarillo, my mother says Winter is right around the corner and she wants to have as many blankets knitted as humanly possible. She says she can tell how harsh the

Winter will be by the colour of the Sun. She says it's going to be a bad one.'

The boy tried to remember how a cold Winter night felt against his face. Breaking his routinary conversation with Pablo, he let a new thought escape his mouth.

'If Winter comes, no matter how harsh, it will be the best thing to ever happen to this town.' Pablo looked puzzled at Lázaro's words, he didn't know that he was living in a village suffering from a perennial Summer. The cursed boy seemed about to react to the change of script when Lázaro concluded the conversation, giving up. 'Yeah, fine, we shall play tomorrow then.'

'I'll come and see you tomorrow morning, I promise. We can go to explore the Gato caves again,' Pablo replied excitedly, oblivious to the curse; unaware that tomorrow would never arrive.

Lázaro couldn't understand how everyone was so compliant about the situation. The boy carried on walking, his mother was waiting.

As he approached the Plaza, he saw that Mr. Fructuoso's

market stall was full of produce, as always. Every potato exactly in the same position it had been since the curse hit the town.

'Hey boy, buy some good lemons for your mum! I'm sure she's cooking something tasty and she may need some. Please, Lázaro - I didn't sell much today, and it's almost night time,' Mr. Fructuoso implored, looking rather desperate.

'Sorry sir, my mother is feeling quite unwell tonight, so we will go to the Mondragón's for dinner time. Thanks though,' said Lázaro, automatically repeating the same lie he used every single time he entered the plaza. It came out so easily now, he was getting quite good at lying, the young boy thought to himself.

Some of the villagers chose not to believe they were cursed. He was not angry at them, in fact, he envied them. He wished he didn't have to bear the burden of awareness. Every other day Lázaro toyed with the idea of inviting the curse into his heart, of giving away control. But he always reached the same conclusion, he was awake to the reality of their world, and he should fight the curse for as long as he had to. He was Ronda's last hope, their last drop of sanity.

The villagers suffered the curse in very different ways. No one grew hungry these days, nor felt any other natural need. They were all stuck, repeating whatever action they were performing when the curse commenced. During the last passing second experienced by humanity. That was it. Frozen in time.

I wish I felt sleepy once again, I wish I felt heavy eyelids and an aching body needing to sleep. If I could, I would sleep for longer than I've been awake. All of these endless years... or perhaps decades. I would sleep the rest of it gladly.

As the boy followed the narrow passages he knew by heart, a monstrous building towered. The Palacio Mondragón, the place where Lázaro's family had been servants for generations. While Lázaro's dad ran the Lord's fields across the region, his mother was the only maid at the Palace, and he would be there to help her... most of the time. He hadn't seen Lord Mondragón since the Sun cancelled its journey behind the sierra. Not that it bothered him, he wasn't a huge fan of the man, the Lord Mondragón was always cold and distant. And he rarely said 'thank you'. He hated that.

Lázaro wasn't work-shy before the curse settled, although he'd abandon any of the dull palace chores at the opportunity of an exciting adventure.

If I must look at the brighter side of the curse, I must admit that I do not miss my life as a servant. There's nothing I miss from inside that palace. Wait! Actually there is, I miss little Talita. I hope she's doing well. He looked at the palace as if he could see through the walls, wondering what the Mondragón's little daughter would be up to. The boy was very protective of her. If it wasn't for the voices of his mother, father and all of his ancestors constantly reminding him to be respectful to the Mondragón and the palace, he would have already broken in and smuggled himself inside its walls to check up on the girl.

Lázaro was adamant about facing the curse. Defying the evil spell of no-time, he constantly introduced little changes that gave him the impression of time passing; closing the blinds and pretending to sleep, changing his off-white linen shirt regularly, and sometimes he would even clean the house. It was a silly thing to do, as it was spotless after the first time the boy cleaned it. Not a speck of dust dared to grace a single item of the stark household. Time kept chores at bay. 'Just imagine mum wakes up and finds me wearing the same clothes we've been wearing for what must have been an eternity. She would definitely kick me right where it stings!' he exclaimed out loud to the empty street, pretending he wasn't alone.

He entered his humble servant's house by the Palace. His mum was still asleep, not that Lázaro held any hope anymore, the boy just missed her. The wet cloth over his mum's forehead was as cold as when he placed it first, still the boy replaced it with a new one. The fever didn't go away. Lázaro covered the windows with curtains, protecting his mother from the dying light and blessing her with the rare comfort of darkness. He kneeled next to his mum and held her hand in his, then the boy talked to her in a caring whisper.

'Mother, don't worry, everything will be ok. We haven't received news from any village around us in quite some time. Father hasn't been back from farming the fields yet. Don't worry mother, the end is near, let's just wait a little bit longer.' After a second of silence, Lázaro climbed into his own bed, pretending to be weary. He closed his eyes, as if to sleep. Only this time something peculiar happened, instead of his mind pondering about the meaning of life, or summoning arguments from the past, hoping for a second chance at winning them - this time, for once, he actually fell asleep.

Somewhere in Ronda, a clock hand in a watchman's pocket almost gathered enough strength to advance one second. One entire second. The first second since the curse started. And one second was all the boy needed to dream. It wasn't the peaceful dream Lázaro was craving. It was a dream full of dreams. The boy stood at the bottom of the cliffs, where the plateau meets the land and the river. A black cat crossed right in front of him and ran deep down into the caves below the city, where the moorish king once lived. Then he saw the ghost. He was the apparition of a very pale man, with bizarre clothes and a thin, black brick in his hands; a brick with a star of its own. As soon as their eyes locked, the ghost began to vanish. The ghost pointed the shining black brick straight at him, a flashing light that seemed to capture his very soul. The thin black brick was adorned with the image of a bitten white apple.

The eerie encounter was interrupted by a voice from the top of the cliff, which somehow felt higher, more daunting, than before. The person was almost stepping on thin air.

'Hey! Hey Lazarillo! You can see the End from here,' the figure crowning the top of the rocks yelled. Lázaro was trying to discern the ominous figure's face, but from the vanishing ghost's black brick, a flashing ray of light shone straight into his eyes, blinding them. The boy shielded his vision trying to define the features of the brave human defying the fatal fall. All he could make out was the man's arm pointing toward the Sun. 'Hey Lazarillo! Look over there my boy,' and the sudden realisation of who the human was struck Lázaro's heart like a lightning bolt.

His father. Raising his hand. Pointing to the horizon.

The young boy turned around, following the finger's target, only to find for once a sunless sky. Only a dark, thin horizon slithered in the distance as if it were alive. Flares of pure darkness jumped towards the sky, and every single living thing succumbed to its depth. Everything the black snake touched, turned into nothing. It was advancing towards Ronda, with a deep hunger, devouring land and beings alike, craving for every living thing to reach their end. To meet a final breath. The land rumbled and unravelled, trying to run away from the destructive horizon. A huge crack opened below the young boy's feet, almost as wide as the cliffs were tall. His body started to float, suspended in air as he observed the scene below. The town of Ronda was about to be swallowed by the fields where it rested.

'Father! Run! Find a way of saving us!' he shouted in despair looking up. His father looked down, and smiling, let his body fall. Jumping head first. Hurtling toward Lázaro at increasing speed. Too late for the boy to dodge the descending progenitor. The boy could see his father's smiling face as it approached him. He covered his head trying to avoid the impact. *Is this my end?*

But then, a miracle. As their bodies were about to clash, time slowed down; all the debris and rocks accompanying his father's body, every crack on the ground, everything that embellished the nightmare, almost came to a halt. Lázaro's father was so close that the boy could clearly see the tears forming in the man's eyes. The boy uncovered his face to look better at his father's. Without losing his smile, the old block met the chip. And as time returned to the dream, the fatal impact sent Lázaro back into the realm of those who were awake.

He hadn't opened his eyes yet, but he could feel the warmth of the Sun against his skin. The promising cold breeze of a night that was never meant to arrive fluttered in the air. The laughter of the three old ladies brought him back to his senses. The pain of the dream still clawed his chest.

The sun, the breeze, the laughter... I'm not in my bed! I must have been sleepwalking through that hellish dream! He thought as he opened his eyes and found himself on the veranda, right at the edge of the cliffs. In the exact location where his father stood in the dream. Shivers ran downthe boy's spine, not distinguishing dream from reality for a second, trying to figure out how he got there. He turned around to step down from the dangerous edge, back into safety, feeling grateful for Ronda to be standing strong over its foundation. The boy looked one last time in the direction of the Sun. His heart stopped and a knot formed in his throat. It was no longer stuff of nightmares.

The mountains in the distance had started to disappear and the horizon turned into a shade of black deeper than the shadows of any cave Lázaro had ever known.

The End was coming.

II - THE BOY

The whole village of Ronda fell silent for just one second. Like the audience in a bullring, right before the bull's horn pierces through a bullfighter. Even the rocks around Lázaro held their breath.

Lázaro found himself confused between despair and hope. He couldn't explain how or why, but he felt he knew the End like he knew himself - there was no doubt that it was approaching, and everything was bound to be consumed by it.

I just want this loop to break, and if salvation takes the disguise of the darkness in the horizon, that darkness cannot come fast enough. He calmed his questioning mind. On one hand, a cold sweat had started to prickle at the back of his neck. His heart was beating at the rhythm of a cantering stallion. He harboured pure fear of the darkness facing him; of nothing existing, of not being himself anymore, of oblivion. On the other hand, he was relieved that there was an end to this existence, after all. The idea of infinite boredom terrified him equally. The boy felt so tired! Not in a way that could be easily resolved by a restful slumber, the tiredness came from the constant rummaging of his mind as it tried to understand the situation and contemplate every possible outcome, each as daunting as the last. *This is stupid, a boy my age should be spending all of his energies on chasing chickens, or daydreaming, lost in worlds that belong in someone's imagination! Here I am dwelling about the pure meaning of life and death!*

The boy sat down on the enormous rock that adorned the cliff, serving as a sentinel guarding the town. A rock that once upon a time belonged to one of the city's main gates - the Wind Gate, now just rubble and growth. Lázaro's eyes did not miss the fine black line, not for one second. The olive trees attached to either side of the rock seemed to ask for a bit of company before the End arrived.

'Am I even alive anymore?' Wondered the little boy out loud, not aware that he was somehow answering to the trees's silent request for conversation. 'What is a life that only waits for the End? No chance, no action... stuck forever in the intention of doing things, never doing them.

Why should I carry on being Lázaro? Why should I wait in Ronda? Are we the only forsaken land in this world?'

The questions flowed from his mouth faster and louder each time, echoing against the rocky walls of Ronda's cliff. The image of his father falling free against his body made the boy stop.

If I can see the End from here, that can only mean that anything West of Ronda must have been obliterated by now. Huelva is towards the West. My father is in Huelva. My father... was in Huelva. The boy thought as tears fought to escape from his eyes. He grabbed a small rock next to him and threw it down the cliff in anger.

'What if my father has met the End already? What if time never comes back? What if I am going to be alone for the rest of my life?' Lázaro broke down, saving his last drops of strength to contain the tears, now about to overflow his eyes. He was exhausted. 'This is not fair! I want to be like the rest of the village! I don't want to feel pain anymore!' He gave in and released the tears. Covering his face, ashamed of being seen in a moment of weakness, he cuddled himself against the old rock. *I wish I could be like this olive tree. I will never be strong enough to fight the curse forever. I am just a lonely kid, completely abandoned and worthless.*

A sudden breeze moved the olive tree leaves and they seemed to pass a secret message to the forlorn boy. Lázaro could have reacted with surprise to the wind, as far as he was aware it had died along with time, but this breeze brought him no comfort. He was too close to giving up for good, and the curse was awaiting its turn to conquer his hopeless heart. The rustling trees provided an answer, and Lázaro, in his weakness, ignored it.

'Who am I kidding, I know the answer. I am as dead as the bones in the old king's grave, for without change, we die.' He said out loud, defying the darkened horizon. Standing up, cleaning the tears from his face with his dirty sleeve, the boy frowned at the End and loudly repeated himself. 'I am dead already. Come and get me, I won't run away!' The curse gained terrain within his heart.

The breeze tried to give him a sign once again and carried a quiet guitar tune from far away directly into his ears. Snapping out of the pesimistic spell, he noticed it. Lázaro stood up trying to find out if he was imagining it. Puffing his chest, he felt enough hope to command the sun to continue its journey, to dispel the curse from the village, to summon the long gone moon, to challenge the End to a race for survival. However, before any of that could take place, his hopes were crushed. The breeze had lost its rebellious power, and a silent landscape was all he had in front of him. Where hope had been, only anger remained. Lázaro was left with tremendous amounts of fury and the newfound knowledge that after all, because he was already dead, he had nothing else to lose. From that point onwards he was free from fear.

Silence got interrupted once again, this time by laughter. *Tasteless laughter.* A sound that woke him up from his existential musings. He had heard that cackling before and he knew exactly which throats it came from. 'Only they would dare to laugh on such a day.' Lázaro muttered angrily, clenching his jaw. He stood up and scrutinised his surroundings like a falcon seeking its prey. The young one felt so offended at the intrusion. *How dare they laugh on the day that I've lost it all. How!? Are they laughing on my father's open grave!? Are they mocking the impending destruction of everything we ever called home!?* The young boy thought as he stomped into the old town, following the cackles. He was a dagger that had been drawn and now claimed its share of blood. Like a bolt, he started to run towards the source of the laughter. Then Lázaro saw them; the three old ladies laughing the day away, unaware that the boy had become one with his grief for the world. *They act and sound younger than myself,* acknowledged Lázaro as he approached the three old piles of skin and bones, trying to contain his built up rage.

'Good Morning, ladies. How's the evening going? It seems like it's gonna be a cold night, shouldn't you go inside and prepare the beds with a couple extra blankets?' Lázaro advised with his fists clenched. He wanted, more than anything, to provoke some form of change in the women. The monotony of their actions made him furious, and there was no more patience inside him. Anger had taken completely over his tiny body.

'Hello young one... we were just remembering the old days, you know? Where men would work the fields properly and the youngsters would break their backs working with their parents...' Maria accused while settling herself deeper into a black shawl. The other two ladies nodded in agreement, as if the young boy knew nothing about the mysteries of adulthood. The vision of the three ladies, covered in their identical widow outfits only made Lázaro angrier.

I can't believe they're acting like the End is not coming! Thought Lázaro, feeling the anxiety growing inside and starting to hinder his ability to breathe.

'Yes, yes, son - blankets! Indeed it feels like it's going to be a chilly night tonight. What have you been up to today, you little imp? Share with us your adventures so our old bones can remember better days.' Perpetua asked.

'Yes, I feel like you've been just walking here and there all day. Why are you not in the fields, helping your dad like a good man?' Eustaquia pointed her finger aimed straight at the boy's heart. The old lady had brought back the painful memory of his dad, and Lázaro felt himself losing grip of his emotions. Being polite by default, like his mother taught him, like his mother expected, the boy answered the question, putting his feelings aside.

'My dad left for Huelva a while ago, he was taking care of

the Mondragón's strawberry fields there. I haven't heard from him in a while...'

'He's left his family alone! The Mondragón! Always the same tale!' Eustaquia cut in, before spitting on the floor, close to Lázaro's feet.

His face darkened at the interruption. *Did my father abandon me? Was I not worth him?* He thought as Eustaquia continued.

'They take, take and take all they want but never give nothing back! Cursed they may be!'

'Eustaquia, Maria, think about what our late husbands would have done. Ha! My Hermenengildo would have taken them out of that palace and put me inside. Like a princess! Ha!' Exclaimed Perpetua, wrapping the black shawl around herself as if it were a dress. The three of them burst into laughter while the boy stood there, shaking with rage. It was time for him to bring change. It was time to open their eyes to the devastating truth of the life they were living.

'Well ladies, in case you haven't noticed-' Lázaro stopped and cleared his throat, he was struggling to dislodge the words from the depths of his body. 'The Sun seems to be frozen in the sky, time has stopped passing and you may as well have been sitting here in this very same position for what could have been centuries. Also, if you look at the horizon...' Explained Lázaro, raising a finger and pointing where the Sun nearly touched the land. 'You'll notice the mountains have started to disappear, because this line of pure nothingness that is approaching our village swallows everything that exists. I saw it in a waking dream. We're all going to disappear.' When Lázaro finished, his heart stopped in anticipation. Up until that point, until the vision of the approaching End, he hadn't even thought of trying anything like that. Sharing the truth, not following up the repetitive conversations. *My father always said I was too polite. Maybe the curse makes us all too polite for our own good. Maybe that's why he left me.* Accepting his advancing end allowed him to push the limits of his own mystery. He looked at the women expecting chaos, but the women stared back at him with wide eyes, as if trying to absorb his words. 'C'mon ladies!' Lázaro said under his breath to himself, praying for change.

'Well, Perpetua...' Eustaquia broke the tense silence, still staring at the boy, attempting to chain one sentence to the next. 'Well, Perpetua...' She repeated, as if she was having problems finding the right words. 'Well, Perpetua, my husband Paco, may he rest in peace, was such an idiot! Oh Lordy! Forgive me for what I'm about to say but, am I happy without him moaning around the house! He was as useless as a stone!' The three ladies started laughing, even louder this time, as if they hadn't registered Lázaro's revelation.

The boy turned around on his heel and ran away, eyes brimming with tears once more. He tried, and he failed. If anything he felt even worse than before, worthless at the thought of everyone abandoning him. The women had ignored anything he said that involved the curse. There wasn't much more he could do at this point.

He continued to run.

'Lazarillo, hijo! Where are you going?! Don't go down there, it's gonna get dark really soon!' The three ladies shouted after him as he left town and began to descend the steps that connected the cliff tops to the land. He decided he would walk a familiar route, towards the Old Mill. It was Lázaro's favourite place outside the cliff town; he loved to hide inside the ruined mill's derelict walls while cooling his feet in the frozen river. There, he would pretend the world didn't exist, and imagine time was flowing as it once did. If only the river was also flowing, the boy's fantasy may have been possible. Instead, the river stayed still below him, flat as a pond.

He ran all the way through farms and into the woods, leaving behind other, less interesting ruins, finally entering the crumbling building that was his home away from home. The trees covering the roofless mill seemed to try and sway in a wind that was not blowing. If he stood in silence and listened hard enough, he swore he could hear the echoes of past conversations, laughter and arguments that once took place when the mill was a functioning mill. Even memories were cursed to be repeated over and over. Lázaro looked at the river ready for the cold reward of the frozen-in-time water. The boy thought, *they say you cannot step twice in the same river! Watch me!* The boy entered the river without finesse, not even taking his clothes or his sandals off. *I can, and I will. I won't wait politely any more. This is my End.* His painful thoughts seemed to ooze from his mind as the water hugged his ankles. Disturbing the motionless river as he moved around, he dreamed of letting himself go; of being taken away to a new land where things changed, where he could grow and become whoever he wanted to become. Once he walked to the middle of the stream, calm surrounded him. In such an alien landscape, he felt safe to unleash his pain. He entered the water until it reached his neck. The silence around him grew thicker, making him feel observed by the nature around him. Trying to break the heavy atmosfear, he screamed. 'I'm tired of the past!' He stared around at the trees expecting them to answer back. Not a single leaf moved. 'I'm also tired of the present!' He shouted as he submerged into the water, holding his breath. He started to swim, imagining that his body was carried by the water down the river until its course met the very End. He imagined finally falling to meet whatever was at the other side of the dark veil. *That would be a nice adventure. Getting to the End rather than waiting for it to get here.* The idea sent shivers down his body, planting a dangerous seed.

As he reached one of the shallows of the river, he paused

his swimming to contemplate this brand new thought. *Getting there before it gets here.* Still within the clear in the woods that held the ruined mill, the boy laid down over a myriad of polished little stones, water barely covering his limbs. Everytime he went to his favourite place, he added a pebble to a carefully crafted pile - little towers populated the river's sandbank. Then, he usually remained in stillness until a thought popped inside his mind. This time, a new plan blossomed from his river trance. Excited, he broke the tranquillity around him with a loud warning to the empty space. 'I want a future! I want change! I will walk to the End and show the villagers of Ronda how it's done! Stop waiting for life to happen, take action, world! You hear me? Do something about it!' The boy jumped into the water once again and swam furiously towards the mill. He exaggerated his movements, trying to turn as much of the river into a splash, into living water following its path towards the sea. Entranced by the desperate ritual, Lázaro tried to kick his leg over the water, not noticing a pointy rock that blocked the movement. He sliced his toe against its sharp edges. The boy released a scream of physical pain

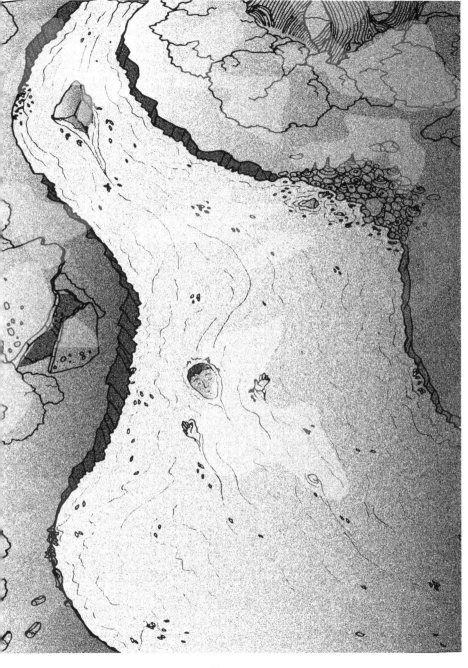

for the first time in forever. He hadn't felt that kind of pain in a long, long while, for time had also stopped the decaying of their bodies. This primal scream did the trick to bother the nature around him and for a split second, the water seemed to rush around him like it once did. The totality of the river rushed down the stream, eager, for the shortest amount of time. The foam of the water against the stones, the sticks and leaves and flowers floating on the surface. The sound of the river embracing his whole body. He was not sure if the piercing pain made him hallucinate, or if time had actually made the waters flow once again. Alarmed, he stood up and looked around, only to find the same oppressive stillness. *Was that real?* He wondered, dragging himself from the water, perplexed. He felt a throb of pain in his toe, and after inspecting it closely he saw something remarkable. From the front of his big toenail a thread of red blood pushed its way to the ground. The boy was bleeding. Dizziness came over him, his own mortality had hit him in the face. *I am not dead after all, neither am I brave enough to walk to the End by myself. I am meaningless in this world, no one will even notice I'm gone. I could never create something new* - he thought, and once the dizzy spell cleared, he was struck with an extremely bad idea. If *I don't want to wait for the End, I can actually create my own.*

Back in Ronda, the young boy climbed the steps. The olive tree, cursed in time, witnessed his steady ascension towards the top of the sentinel rock. Lázaro was not aware, but the tree remembered the ancient times when that very rock formed part of the Wind Gate, allowing merchants and visitors to enter the city. This was a long time ago, when the Arabs ruled the region. Lázaro reached the same place from his dream, the same place from which his dad had fallen. From that place he could see absolutely everything. The New Town of Ronda, with its majestic Bullring, the majestuous orange stone bridge and everything in-between the furious End and himself. 'Why wait until the End gets here when I can meet my own end right here, right now?' He repeated, trying to convince himself as he took tiny steps towards the edge of the cliff. He was ready to give up one last time. He was ready to jump. Teetering on the edge, Lázaro gave himself one last chance to take the beautiful scenery in, searching the horizon for an excuse to stop himself. But the truth was that everything he could see only brought him more pain. More fear. The End relished at the thought of what was about to happen.

Just one last step.

A last thought wandered into the mind of Lázaro, not an unusual occurrence for those about to die. Looking at the rocks around him, he felt sympathy. *Without Time, there's no real difference between this stone and myself.* At first it struck him like deja vu, but then his awareness expanded, and through pure compassion he became aware of every sentient being around him, below and above. For a fleeting moment, he was one with them, the grass, the trees, the rocks and the skies. His eyes were everywhere, he felt roots, wings and crystals all around him. He was them, they were him. And only then he began to understand. *That's all we are now, our awareness means nothing without Time. Nothing matters anymore, this is the end of the world. Although, if there's an end, that means there must be a beginning somewhere after that terrible curtain. If I believe in the nothingness before my eyes, I must believe that there is something right after it.* A tiny spark of hope tried to ignite within the boy's heart, but he continued to think, as his consciousness re-focussed into his body. With a loud hum covering his ears, the boy became singular once again. He felt more alone than ever before. *Who am I kidding? The differences between me and stone are meaningless now. Nothing can bring change into this world, ever again. I might as well be a rock. A tree. A blade of grass. We are the same against the End. We wait, and for we wait, we die... I don't want to wait anymore. I don't want to be alone anymore.* Lázaro mouthed, as if in a trance. Against the philosophical defeat, hope abandoned the boy's heart, lost for good. He closed his eyes and shifted his weight slowly, about to meet his own end.

As his eyelids met, the boy caught some unnatural movement in the road below. Abruptly shaken, the boy took a step back from the edge. *What is that?* The boy ran through every possibility in his head, but birds were not flying anymore, not a soul in Ronda got stuck roaming the roads endlessly, and the movement came from a figure too big for it to be a stray cat or dog. It was calmly traversing through the road leading to Ronda, the size of an ant at the boy's naked eye. *Is that - a man?* Lázaro couldn't place the figure, he recognised nothing about him, but there was definitely a man walking towards the town of Ronda. A man carrying a big traveller hat that covered his face, with tired steps from a long and exhausting journey. The first visitor since the curse took over the villagers.

'Father!?' Lázaro shouted into the still air as he dangerously approached the edge of the cliff. His own voice surprised him with desperation. The boy looked down and saw the imminent drop. Vertigo. The fear took control of his legs and made him walk backwards, falling into his rear with his eyes wide open. *I can't believe I was about to-* the young one thought, unable to articulate the sinful act he barely avoided. *As long as I breathe, every time air fills my lungs, I will bring change. And I will choose to confront the End at any opportunity I'm given. Even if I have to do it all alone.* He raised his eyes towards the horizon and stared at the raging End in disgust. 'Nope, not today.' He muttered for the rocks and the olive tree, the only witnesses of his original intention, before regaining some composure. The boy looked carefully, the stranger still walked towards Ronda. As Lázaro stood up, he pondered carefully what his next move would be. *It may not be my father, I better be cautious. Not a good time to trust strangers.* And so the boy decided to take the stairs to descend, which would take longer than jumping off the cliff, but it was definitely a safer option.

III - THE TRAVELLER

In which a shadow gets scared; a builder spits; a guitar rests;
and Lorenzo meets the devil.

Lorenzo walked through the Sierra for what felt like years before he laid his eyes on the cliffs of Ronda. The traveller felt the ominous light of the dying titan sun against his skin and he found himself smiling for the first time since his journey started.

The mountains were a very dangerous place during the twilight. They seemed endless, and passing through them was an arduous task. At every step, he had to test where his feet were landing before placing the rest of his weight on the treacherous edges. The traveller thanked himself for not packing much other than a simple wooden guitar. The instrument was his loyal friend, who had accompanied him through the darkness of the mountain edges and valleys. The monumental peaks appeared to be judging the traveller, trying to set barriers to his escape. Rearranging their walls in a living maze that didn't want him to be free. The whole land moved at a continental speed, trying to avoid the ruinous End itself.

During his travels across the ungrateful Sierra, Lorenzo had grown used to silence. Birds did not sing anymore, and the only ones he came across were corpses being devoured by the alms of the earth forever more; eternally decomposing, never fully becoming one with the soil. The silence joined the grey mountain walls in quiet threat, one that accused him of leaving his home instead of waiting for the End, like everyone else. Lorenzo had a remedy for this isolation. When he felt as if he couldn't take another second, he carefully uncovered his wooden guitar from his light backpack and sang for the mountains. A few chords that bounced wall to wall, filling the space for miles, almost indicating the way through the twilight.

When the sound reached back to the traveller, Lorenzo felt that his music brought the untold stories of the rocks; the things they had seen, from a past long gone. The Sierra stood alert, listening to the wanderer's prayers of mercy and remorse. Lorenzo couldn't stop thinking about his grandmother. In an ocean of suffering, her image brought him the deepest pain, the sharpest sorrow he'd ever known. Grief.

As the great bridge of Ronda appeared on the horizon, Lorenzo hoped he wouldn't have to break the news to the inhabitants of the cliff city. He wondered if the people there waited, or if they were busy trying to prevent the imminent ending. He did not know that a child was taking action, ready to jump off the highest part of the city walls, and break every single bone in his body against the ancient rocks at the base of Ronda.

Lorenzo started his ascending path toward the town, unable to move his gaze from the labyrinthic plateau in front of him. The pebbled slope had welcomed many traders, workers and visitors with both good and evil intentions.

Ronda was a garden of splendour in bygone days, disputed by multiple conquerors, it now remained a dusty palace on top of some unkempt cliffs. The white houses reflected the orange sun's spell, and almost merged with the rock that hosted them. The Moorish walls reminded Lorenzo that this region was once the wealthy throne of North African princes and princesses, all gone way before the End appeared on the horizon he had left behind. He thought about his mother. He wondered if this was the very path

she had followed, carrying him tightly as they both left Ronda for good; the town in which he was born.

As he walked the path to get to the city, he came across a man working on the enormous legs of the imposing Great Bridge. This was the wanderer's opportunity to discover if the curse had extended to other towns, or if it was only the one he came from that had been unlucky.

'Hey! You, working over there! Could you spare a few moments to give a lost visitor some directions?' Lorenzo shouted, shuddering when he heard the echo of his own voice filling the mighty structure. The worker looked at him without stopping his endeavours.

'Huh, I'm busy can't you see? This bridge is not gonna keep herself up y'know? It's been my job for the past thirty years, and before that it was my parents' job, and before that it was my father's parents job, and after me, it'll be my daughter's, y'know? Give us a second and I'll be with ya.' Grunted the man. Lorenzo saw the builder working on top of the most precarious scaffolding he could imagine. A tower of cane that swung one way to another at every small movement the builder made.

'Aren't you scared of heights, good man? You are so high up it's making me feel dizzy.' Lorenzo overreacted, trying to avoid looking down to the canyon below them.

'Nah kiddo, since I was born my parents used to hang me here and there, y'know? A man from a cliffed city shouldn't be scared of heights! Now quick, tell me, what brings you to Ronda? We're not fond of strangers around here.' The man started applying some grey paste to the tiny cracks in the stone in front of him.

'I am looking for the Mondragón. Would you know where I could find them?' The wanderer asked, timidly. The builder grunted, without stopping his work.

'You must be crazy if you wanna see Lord Mondragón... salty pig he is.' He cursed and spat down to the river.

Lorenzo was disgusted at the action. Even when the traveller's family was far from wealthy, the women in his family made sure he was educated enough not to spit around. The mouthful hit the surface of the river below them, with such an aim, that the impact broke the silence within the canyon.

Silence. The traveller noticed the silence, and his fears went wild. *There is a river flowing underneath the bridge, the waters should be quite loud as they fall from rock to rock.* He approached the edge of the pathway overlooking the bottom of the cliffs.

The water was not flowing.

The curse had reached this corner of the world as well. *There's no escape.* From that point, the wanderer didn't hear a single direction the builder was giving him, for despair had filled him whole. No matter how far he ran away, the whole world was on hold, waiting for whatever had destroyed his village to hit this one as well. *I have to keep on moving,* he thought, letting desperation take control. In his shock and without saying goodbye, Lorenzo walked his way up to the old town.

'Ungrateful youth, ungrateful stranger.' The builder growled as he saw the traveller turn around and leave. He spat again, this time hitting the ground where Lorenzo had been standing a moment ago.

When Lorenzo reached the top of the cliffs, the town spilled in front of him. He was in no mood to appreciate the charm of the cursed settlement. However, the sound of heavy footsteps wrenched him from his dread. By the sound of it, someone was running manically. As he came back into his senses and looked in the direction from which the footsteps were coming from, he found nothing. An empty street. *Just what we need, ghosts on top of the imminent end,* thought Lorenzo, feeling hopeless and deflated. The traveller wasn't the most pious of humans, but he did respect the souls of the gone, and most importantly, wanted nothing to do with them.

Memories of the destruction of his town flashed before his eyes. Lorenzo wondered if the eastern mountains between his town and Ronda would be strong enough to protect them from utter destruction. *Let's see, I'm leaving Alpandeire behind, that's to the East. If I keep running West, following the road to Huelva, I may escape the darkness that swallowed my village. But before that, let's resolve all of my unfinished business. I need to find my father.* The traveller thought to himself, completely oblivious to the reach of the evil horizon.

He walked until he found a square with a few benches and a

fountain with eight openings, an arrangement of green and blue frogs with gaping mouths that no longer produced water. 'Another reminder that everything is broken.' He exhaled as he sat on one of the benches looking into the city, his knees cracked loudly after a lifetime of navigating through the steep mountains. His body was so relieved, a pleasurable wave of pins and needles covered his lap. Once he was comfortably sitting, he pushed his bag and guitar to one side, gently resting the instrument against the trunk of an orange tree next to him. The orange blossoms above him kept the sunlight away, providing some solace, distracting the man from noticing the western mountains starting to disappear. The rows of white limestone houses surrounded the square as if they were scrutinising the intruding man. The windows became prying eyes, the statues of saints murmured gossip to each other, the broken frogs held their breath. Lorenzo was a stranger in Ronda, and the town was making it known to him. He felt uneasy sitting there, vulnerable. He could almost feel someone, or something, following his every move. *If this town ends up being a town filled with the dead, I am going to pass out.* Lorenzo promised to himself, scared to the bone marrow. He could no longer sit idle, so he began to wander again, hoping to stumble into the Mondragón and their infamous palace.

His guitar stayed behind.

He got lost quite quickly. Every single street looked the same way to him. The further into town he ventured, the more the air pressed heavily against him. The sun, so distant from the dinginess of the streets, illuminated the pink and orange sky above them. There was a darkness Lorenzo could not see, but sense, inside the old walls of the houses. The structures had been witnesses to years and years of humanity, and now they braced themselves for the End. They could feel it creeping and reducing the living realm to dust, so they secured their sinful secrets within their rooms and under their floor boards, hoping for the abominable dark horizon not to unveil them.

In the dark and surrounded by stone, Lorenzo couldn't help but notice a drop in temperature, he felt weakened as the cold wormed its way into his bones. He started praying by default, asking his grandmother in heaven to give him strength to find the way out from the cursed town. The misty darkness in front of him grouped into a solid small being; a four legged nightmare unfolding in front of his eyes.

This is it, a demon is here to claim my soul. This is exactly what my grandmother said would happen if I sinned. Here I am, meeting my end like the coward I am! He continued to pray in fear, as he was about to faint.

Then, the traveller saw them, two little glowing orbs, shining amidst the darkness. As the daemonic gaze approached Lorenzo, the man prayed louder. When the demon saw the crying man, a high hiss rang in the air. *I've tried my best, Lord, I promise!* In front of him, the forbidden demon appeared; a black cat exposing a huge puffy tail. The cat was as frightened as Lorenzo. With expert agility, the feline bolted down the street, back into the shadows. *Just a cat. It was just a cat! Thank you grandma.* He thanked looking upwards. *I am so sorry, I am such a coward. Really sorry, I promise I will make my journey count.* He leaned against the cold stone of a nearby house, breathing once more, relieved that no demons visited him.

Wait. Animals have been acting weirdly since the curse

began, this cat was different! Realised Lorenzo, turning around to catch a glimpse of the black tail as it disappeared around a corner. Hopeful, the man began to race after the cat, dodging the corners of the houses tracing the streets, every turn more chaotic and narrower than the last.

Lorenzo halted and looked around but the cat was nowhere to be found. He had managed to get himself deeper in the darkest part of the cursed town. Then, a crude scream slashed the air, so high-pitched that Lorenzo's blood ran cold. He knew he was in trouble as a thin white mist started to cover the pavement. Lorenzo knew, deep down, that no living woman, man or animal could have been the source of such a terrible sound. *This time there's no doubt. A ghoul.* Foretold the stranger as he avoided making any sound that could give away his location. The mist continued to roll in; then the deepest silence, followed by the voice of a woman. 'Anyone! Help me, anyone! Please, I beg of you!' the lady screamed for help desperately, as loud as she could.

Lorenzo turned towards the direction the screams were coming from. *Someone needs my help, and as terrifying as ghouls are, I have been raised by wonderful women to be a good Roman Catholic Apostolic human. Please grandma give me strength to be brave!* He tried not to think as he weaved his way through the stone maze towards the lady in peril.

After stumbling around a corner, he finally saw her dark figure. With no time for his eyes to adjust to the eerie vision, the figure dissolved into thin air. Lorenzo had no idea what was going on. He approached the place where the lady had freshly been, looking for any clues about the twisted mirage, when another scream came from a different direction.

'Please! Anyone! Help me, I beg of you!' The same inconsolable voice summoned aid once again. Lorenzo didn't think twice about it before attending to the lady's request. I *will prove to everyone I'm not that much of a coward anymore!* He ran with all of his might, not really understanding anything that was taking place around him. The walls of Ronda observed the situation full of empathy for the lost stranger; he wouldn't be the first soul put to sleep by the spirits that the End had unleashed on Earth. Lorenzo continued to feel his way through the darkness once more, seeking the source of the voice. There she was again, amidst the growing darkness, begging for help. Lorenzo approached the woman, only for her to vanish once more. Her extraordinarily long arms remained for a moment, before they too merged with the stale air. Again, the ghost screamed somewhere not far from him. Lorenzo ran, more cautiously this time, muttering a prayer.

The streets were covered by a sudden night that presented no relief from the lacerating eternal sunlight, for it was clearly unholy. The scared traveller could see nothing around him, so he extended his arms, trying to find a wall in the dark to guide his steps. Instead of the hard and cold stone, his hand met something soft and cushioned. He pushed against its resistance, and his hand was swallowed into the dark in front of his eye. The softness he felt with his cloaked hand divided itself between his fingertips, a familiar feeling of falling asleep while playing with his mother's hair. It was too late, he was inside a thick mane of the darkest curls. Lorenzo screamed in desperation while trying to recover his hand from the treacherous threads. Trying to find a point of support to push his hand out of the woman's hair, he started to feel the features of a face with skin as cold as marble. When he touched the soft lips, they opened.

'Please! I beg you! Forgive me mother for I have sinned! Allow me up there in Heaven and I will be your humble servant!' The scream that followed deafened Lorenzo, as he joined the screams in hysterical response.

Grandma this is my end, please make sure the doors of heaven are open and ready to take me. Prayed Lorenzo as the lady disappeared. His hand now released, reaching out to the empty space. A dim light appeared around him as the mist vanished. His hand was now pointing to a stone statue, atop a little altar adorned with flickering candles. The eerie shadows the flames projected covered the whole temple, crowned by the beautiful figurine of a dark virgin, dressed up in an ostentatious garment. His heart was beating so fast he thought it was going to give up. The presence of the virgin only meant to Lorenzo that he was safe now. Below the statue, a beautifully written text identified the figure as 'The Lady of Our Sorrows.' The traveller scanned around the surrounding buildings, ensuring the ghoul wasn't creeping around. From another building's window, the sounds of someone cooking a puchero stew filled the air with a heavy aroma. The mist overflowed the nearby alleys, but the stranger was in sacred grounds now, he could rest. An extension of the roof from one of the houses created a shelter-like place for devotion right in the streets. 'Who would want their virgin to live in the streets?' He whispered to the holy effigy. His eyes followed the intricate carvings that raised into a golden vault resembling a starry night. 'If only I could see the stars once again... If only I could see my grandmother again,' he lamented to the virgin. The eyes of the traveller continued their journey through the strange architecture. Behind him, two columns held the temple strong. A set of four human-like figures adorned the stone pillars, they were tied by a carved rope at neck height, with bulging eyes, struggling to breathe. The sight tormented Lorenzo. *So much pain in such a little town. I will make my family proud by kneeling down and praying for these lost soul's sins. Then I will leave this place forever, and carry on running away, towards the West, away from the End,* the stranger thought as he kneeled to mutter a heartfelt prayer to the lady of the shrine.

A hand touched his shoulder.

Lorenzo screamed, expecting the ghoul to reappear demanding his soul, falling on his back and crawling away from the devil. Instead, a skinny boy looking abandoned stood there, frowning.

'Welcome to the shrine of Our Lady of Sorrows, stranger' said Lázaro firmly, shadows cast from the curseless flickering candles, danced across their faces. 'What are you doing in Ronda?'

The traveller observed the tiny boy; *worn out shoes, worn out clothes - is this a real boy, or am I being fooled by the ghosts of this forsaken village?* Wondered Lorenzo, trying to regain his adult demeanour. The boy looked taller than he was as he loomed over the traveller, scrutinising the terrified soul, awaiting for an answer. Lorenzo knew he had to tread lightly, and so containing his fear, he met the boy's gaze. *Those are not the eyes of the cursed.* They thought about each other.

The light behind Lázaro's eyes presented a mystery to the traveller. *A mystery I am not going to try and decipher.* He

thought as a feeling of safety invaded his mind. It was the first time Lorenzo had stopped running away for a long time. *Oh Grandma, have I arrived at my destination?* In the middle of the suffocating streets and under the protection of the Lady of the Sorrows, the uninvited presence of the puzzling boy felt like home to the traveller. Not knowing why, his lips parted. First a tiny whisper, promptly a manly voice, Lorenzo started talking, revealing more information than he would have wanted.

'My name is Lorenzo, I'm from Alpandeire, on the other side of the Sierra. To the East from here. I came to Ronda looking for the Mondragón.' Lorenzo said, trying to control a voice that was still recovering from the encounter with the ghoul. The boy didn't answer, so Lorenzo continued talking. 'You are not cursed are you? I did not know there were other people out there... Do you know why this is happening?'

Lázaro's heart skipped a beat at the mention of the curse. Something inside his chest began to expand in pain and freedom. Only now he saw the traveller's face clearly. The stranger's hat had blocked the boy's view during his sneaky chase around Ronda: the tired way in which the stranger walked, the big hands, the locks of dark blonde hair appearing underneath the hat, every little detail kept Lázaro's hope alive. *How did I think you could have been my father?* The boy thought, disappointed; the small forehead, young nervous eyes, big arched nose and incipient stubble in front of him revealed a completely different reality. *I need to play this cool. He may be the change I have been waiting for! But he also may be a spawn of hell, controlled by a witch, or worse, a witch himself!* Thought the hyped boy, trying to assess if the stranger presented a threat to the cursed people of Ronda.

'Well in that case you must be either a hero or a fool, which one of those are you, Lorenzo?' The boy pushed, interrogating the stranger lying on the floor. 'How did you even cross the Sierra? It must be very dark there.' The boy said, not fully believing that the weak-looking stranger in front of him had achieved such a task during the twilight. Lorenzo had never been really good with confrontation, but he was not going to pass the opportunity to talk to someone like him. *I need to learn as much as I can from this boy, if we want to escape this horrible situation we're stuck with. I better stay on his good side... for now.*

'I must have spent months, even years, one step at a time. Carefully avoiding any fall, and soothing myself with the company of my guitar. Alpandeire was cursed, and so was everyone in there.' Lázaro looked at the stranger in awe, he was starting to believe his unlikely story. At that precise moment, Lorenzo remembered his grandma. The memory of him meeting the End, made him shiver in fear. The traveller had prayed and prayed to find someone aware of the absence of time, but now that he had finally found someone, it was too late, fear had taken absolute control of his body. *Change of plans,* he resorted. *I do not need to learn anything from anyone, I am the only person I should be taking care of.* He stood up, and looked at the boy right in the eye. 'Something evil is coming this way. If you are as cheeky as you look, my boy, you should leave this place. Now.' He said before turning away and starting to walk toward the outer streets of the old town of Ronda. The traveller chose to run away, like he had been doing since the curse had started.

Lázaro stood still, trying to make sense of his thoughts as he watched the stranger leave. His father was gone, his mother was ill and the End was coming. *So why am I smiling? This stranger changes everything. Nothing has happened for as long as I can remember and now here he stands. I cannot let him go, I need to know more.* Lázaro thought, detecting the smell of a heroic quest in the frozen wind. The boy ran to catch up with Lorenzo. His wide smile, accompanied by relieving thoughts. *May this stranger be a robber after the Mondragón's fortune, a fool or a hero... Does it matter anymore? Now that the End is this close? I'll embrace the risks and follow him in his journey. At the very least, it will keep boredom away.* Lázaro was catching up to the traveller, ready for the first adventure those lands had seen since time stopped.

'Let's start anew, stranger! I'm Lázaro! Welcome to Ronda!' The boy shouted as he reached the man, . He couldn't contain all the thoughts and questions that had been brewing inside him for as long as he could remember. 'Have you noticed the sun stopped a while ago? People also seem to have gotten stuck in time, doing the same thing over and over. What is your business with the Mondragón? Do you think this is a spell by an evil witch? My mother says they are real and they kidnap people in their sleep.' Lázaro became a boy again. Voicing his ideas was igniting a fireplace in a house that had been cold and empty for too long. 'Can you feel something evil approaching, as well?'

Lorenzo hadn't been with someone freed from the curse for so long, that all this sudden chatter gave him an incipient headache. The mention of the approaching terror made his legs feel weak. If pure fear didn't control his limbs, taking him as far away as they could, he would have curled up on the floor and cried until his body was gone. He had to keep on trying to escape the approaching horizon. He didn't want to get stuck taking care of a lost child, filled with questions he wasn't ready to tackle yet. *I cannot let down anyone else, I cannot be myself around the kid. I need to think of a way to leave him behind.* The idea of becoming all alone frightened him equally. Two conflicting fears fought within the traveller over the direction of his journey. *Shall I run away from the horizon? Or should I keep him by my side as the horizon catches up with us?*

Lázaro awaited a reply expectantly, looking at the man with eyes that denoted admiration.

Lorenzo's fear of being by himself won the battle by quickly weaving an excuse into his speech. *Maybe he can take me to the Mondragón palace... I could meet my father and then leave. That way I'd keep the boy around for as long as he's useful. And then I will continue to run away.* Lorenzo thought strategically before he kickstarted his misleading plan.

'Hello, my boy, I just want to say goodbye to the Mondragón before I carry on with my journey, as they were close family friends.' The traveller explained, his fear easing as the rays of sun began to appear through the architectural mess. 'Do you know where I could find the palace? I'd hate to get caught with one of those ghosts again-' Lorenzo's voice trembled a bit at the mention of the lost soul. *Damn it Lorenzo! Keep it together!* - the traveller scolded himself.

Lázaro nodded, he knew exactly what the stranger meant by ghosts. He had spent too long walking around town, and he was careful to avoid those cold spots filled with sorrow and thick mist. The excited boy over-shared his knowledge of cursed Ronda. 'She was an Anima, not a ghost' Replied Lázaro, deeply saddened by the thought of poor christian souls not finding peace in their promised paradise. 'We have lots of them if you go deep enough into town, where the mist covers the floor. They wander in horrible pain. The doors to Heaven remain closed, now that the doors to Hell seem to be open right in front of our faces.' Lorenzo, puzzled by the boy's words, wondered if Lázaro had seen the greedy horizon of death and despair. *He said he can feel something coming like I do, but in order to lay eyes upon it, he must have been on the other side of the Sierra as the End is coming from the East.* The traveller tried to understand how Ronda knew about the End but his thoughts got interrupted by the boy. Lázaro changed the subject, noticing that the traveller was going a tad pale. 'I know the Mondragón really well, although I haven't seen them since all of this started. Follow me Lorenzo, I'll take you to them.' The traveller nodded, keeping in character, hiding his fears. *One quick stop, then I'll be on my way.* And the pair turned around, away from the sun, never witnessing the End gaining groung from the West.

IV - THE PALACE

In which Lázaro plays hide and seek; soup is almost had; and a wife sticks to what she knows.

'Are you close to Lord Mondragón, then? Is he a good man?' Enquired Lorenzo, trying to find out more about the rulers of the area.

Strolling by a row of orange trees, the unusual pair forgot about the impending doom, allowing themselves to focus on the little things that make life worth living ; such as gossip.

'The patron always rewards hard work but he also knows how to remind you of where you stand. He's kind of fair to my dad. Although I've caught my mum gossiping about him a couple times - apparently he needs to learn how to treat a woman, before he can even think of becoming a good leader.' Lázaro recalled, missing his mother.

Lorenzo nodded in silent agreement, then added with a hint of remorse. 'Yes, I've heard a couple things myself. He is a bit of a twat. How come you know so much about the landlord?'

'Well, because everyone in town talks about them. But also

because my family has been working for the Mondragón since I was born. My dad is actually taking care of their orchards in Huelva. Mother is their maid. I was raised in that palace so I know every single cobweb, portrait and golden leaf hanging on its walls. Have you ever seen the palace before?' They were walking through the Old town of Ronda, meandering through the white fortress.

The traveller sighed. 'Yeah. Kind of, I guess? I was born there, but as you can imagine, I don't remember much.' Lorenzo blushed, he hadn't talked about his Mondragón origins to anyone before, it slipped off his tongue. *Hopefully he didn't pick it up.* Lorenzo prayed in silence as Lázaro readied himself with further questions about the stranger's revelation.

Lorenzo's anxiety started to climb from his stomach up to his heart. To counter whatever the curiosity emanating from the boy, he had to think of something. Random questions piled in his head, until one of them popped out from his mouth. 'Has it been raining ash in Ronda? We had the strangest weather in Alpandeire.' Spurred Lorenzo, hoping it would pique the boy's interest enough to forget about the details of his birth.

'Woah! We haven't had that at all! Here we just have people stuck in time... Maybe there's some sort of spell? I am not a silly little kid, I don't believe in witches.' He lied, shivering as he pronounced the dreaded word. 'But anything can happen these days. I'm just saying we should prepare ourselves to fight a witch.' As soon as Lázaro said it, he felt embarrassed by his naive reasoning. After all this time, although his body had not aged a day, his mind didn't belong to that of a child - not anymore. He should be doing better. 'My mother is very ill, you see, so I didn't want to leave her side for too long-' Lázaro felt a knot forming in his throat. All of these feelings, bottled up for centuries, fought against his body to be released.

'Sorry to hear about your mother, but what do you mean you couldn't leave? Is there anywhere else you need to be?' Lorenzo followed up, not noticing that the boy was starting to tremble.

I need to control my emotions. I cannot appear weak to the stranger. Lázaro thought as he took a deep breath. 'If my mother hadn't been ill I would have been brave like you, that's what I mean. I would have left Ronda and walk toward-'

'Don't worry, my boy, I understand how difficult it is to leave behind the ones you love.' Lorenzo interrupted him pretending to be in control. Guilt loomed, bird of prey over a warm corpse. 'Don't worry, honestly. You're young, there will be plenty of days and years for you to explore the world!' Lorenzo stopped talking as he understood how stupid the suggestion was. Lázaro stared blankly back at him for a moment, catching up to his silly comment. Both exploded in laughter so loudly that they almost fell on their backs. They had forgotten how good laughing felt. Time was the only thing they didn't have. But thanks to its absence, this moment of rare happiness felt eternal, endless. For as long as they laughed, the End was forgotten.

But Ronda was in a rush and the Mondragón palace appeared in front of them, stone cold, expecting them to proceed with their story. The two towers at either side made them feel rather uneasy. The palace had been shut tight since the day Time had disappeared, and now they were about to disturb the peaceful atmosphere. *Only ghosts from the past could live there.* Thought Lorenzo, impressed at the size of the palace. Lázaro knocked thrice on the gigantic wooden door by using a metallic door knob; melted and shaped by ancient hands, shaped as a textured leaf. It was so heavy that he had to use both his hands to lift it. As it hit the solid block of wood, the low rumbling noise it caused echoed towards the depths of the building, but also the depths of their hearts. Ronda seemed annoyed at the disturbance, a small earthquake that no one felt had taken place.

The answer to the knocking on the door was a simple high pitched screech, coming from one of the windows scraping open above. A tiny head appeared behind the metallic bars protecting the palace's riches. Lázaro instantly recognised the female figure; Ana Beatriz, the Portuguese carer for the Mondragón's only child, little Talita. The childminder spoke from the heights.

'Is that you, Talita?'

'No, Ana Beatriz, it's Lazarillo, from next door.' Lázaro replied, and the woman sighed in frustration.

'What do you need, *rapaz*? I can't find the girl and the patron is already sitting at the table, expecting dinner. I have no time to waste with your little things. Your mum didn't show up today so I've been swamped with work.'

'We need to talk to the patron, it's urgent, you see?' The boy didn't want to shout too much, the authority the palace inflicted on him demanded respect. He had to be polite.

'She must be hiding somewhere in her room, I'm busy now, *rapaz*. Use the back door like you usually do, I'll announce you to the patron in a second.' Ana Beatriz disappeared with urgency, but before she closed the window she gave Lázaro and the traveller some advice. 'It better be urgent. You should know better than showing up at dinner time. He won't want to be interrupted.' The screech of the window closed the conversation.

Lázaro wondered if they had fallen victims to the curse, hopeful that perhaps the palace's walls were thick enough to offer protection. 'Shall we try the back entrance then, Lorenzo?' Lázaro asked, walking toward the plaza on one side of the palace. The little square seemed to dance under the light of the orange sun. A solitary tree and a few humble houses contrasted with the nobility of the royal building.

'That's my house, the one in the corner. My mum is in there, resting.' The boy felt the sting of not being good enough. *What is he going to think about us? This traveller probably pictures us as servants without a will or power.* 'My dad is actually very important to Lord Mondragón. He doesn't just take care of all the patron's strawberry orchards back in Huelva, he also sells them even to the far North. The nicest ones in all of the land, they say.' Bragged the boy before giving Lorenzo a tour around a place that felt like his own backyard. After all, he had grown up here, watching his mum take care of the big palace. He had learned how to crawl through the fancy gardens and grand corridors, and later on, how to walk. Lorenzo was listening, but he was too distracted fearing whatever he was about to encounter inside the palace.

'Mother would water every single planter,' the boy continued. 'Always saying nice things to them so they would grow stronger. She did lots of stuff around the palace grounds. She is the best mother. You'll see when you meet her-' Lázaro stopped himself, realising that sadly, he won't have a chance to make those introductions.

'Is your mum...?' Lorenzo dared to ask, anticipating the

worst.

'She was very ill when the sun stopped.' Lázaro cut him off. 'She's still ill, the fever won't go down no matter what I try. It's likely that she will be sleeping forever.' He felt the knot coming back, strangling his voice, so he hurried to unbolt the door. Quickly, they gave themselves to the cold embrace of the palace. It was refreshing to find some shelter from the sun, and the fading sky that hung with permanent threat above them. Lorenzo didn't ask any more questions. He understood too well the pain of seeing a mother wither.

They walked in the dark until their eyes adjusted to their gloomy surroundings. The boy knew the maze-like interior of the palace by heart, Lorenzo however, couldn't tell where he was anymore. All the corridors looked alike in the low light. Big doors stood ajar, hinting at comfortable rooms, where imposing portraits of former commanders observed them from behind every corner. Arabic-inspired tea rooms with dozens of colourful cushions succeeded one after the other, endless carpets and a golden tea sets glistened in the twilight, as they weaved their way through the palace.

They reached a wide opening at the end of a corridor, and Lorenzo knew he was at the heart of the palace. The main dining room, a large and exuberant space, decorated to impress visitors and enemies alike. It was as if a once-buried memory reminded him that he had just entered his own home, and he found himself looking up. The Arabic past of the palace boasted the best of their crafts. Wooden motifs embellished the vaulted ceiling, following precise geometrical patterns that were adorned with gold, dark blue and white. Lorenzo noticed how different these fake stars looked compared to those in the Virgin's shrine. A sky studded with stars that were forbidden to be witnessed forevermore. The smell of the ancient wood imbued the room with an air of tradition, strength and honour.

The traveller's eyes followed the patterns carefully, looping with the snake-like golden ribbons that twisted around the entrance's pillars. There were no suffocating men carved into these columns, instead, beautiful leaves of gold bloomed in every angle. They guided Lorenzo's gaze toward the base of the wood, and that's when he saw them. At the back of the room, straight under the far end of the vault, a perfectly laid table stood untouched. Lorenzo would never know it, but he was born on top of that very table. It was long, draped with white linen and covered with beautiful *cartuja* crockery; coral, blue and porcelain. A fully lit candelabra cast its glow over two figures, sat opposite one another at each end of the lengthy dinner table. Both sat in silence, waiting. Lorenzo, succumbing to the pressure of being in the presence of Lord Mondragón, felt the panic building up within his body.

Lázaro cleared his throat before disturbing the scene.

'Dear patron, so sorry to interrupt your dinner. It's Lázaro. I'm here because this man, Lorenzo, wants to talk to you about the day he was bor-' but before he could finish, Lorenzo pulled the boy's arm and whispered urgently in his ear.

'Boy, what are you doing? I cannot do this. I can't! Get us out of here!'

Lázaro, startled, saw that Lorenzo was pale, with a face covered in droplets of sweat that had begun to crawl profusely down his brow. Something wasn't right.

'Look, stranger,' Lázaro replied in a frantic whisper. 'You

made me sneak into my patron's house, interrupt their dinner and all of that for nothing?! My mum could get fired, or worse, they could even banish us! It wouldn't be a first for them.'

Lorenzo looked at him, eyes wide open in fear. The both of them stared at each other in silence. Lázaro, as terrified as he was of being banished by the Mondragón, was hit by a realisation. 'Life as we know it is gone, no one is going to fire anyone.' Knowing that he had nothing to lose, Lázaro readjusted his posture and proceeded to lie to the patron.

'This man here works with my father in your Huelva's strawberry orchards. He says the work over there has finished for the season, and he would like for everyone to be granted permission to return to their families.'

Lázaro felt Lorenzo relax beside him. They expectantly waited for the response with bated breath. In that silence, every tiny sound could be heard, even the efforts of the frozen little candle flames, trying to overcome the curse, flickering away in the heavy air.

A voice deeper than the mines below them; a voice like a good wine that had long been fermenting inside a closed mouth, spilled and reverberated through the room.

'Lázaro, that is great news indeed.' It boomed, 'you interrupt nothing, we haven't even started yet. Talita is playing hide and seek. Ana Beatriz went to find her not a minute ago. Why don't you go give her a hand? Talita's always liked you. In the meantime, Lorenzo, join us for dinner, we can talk about the orchards in detail.' Lord Mondragón didn't ask, he commanded and Lorenzo obeyed.

Behind such a voice there was a jaded body; one that belonged to a general who had fought one too many wars. The patron's remaining hair shone under the light, flattened and stretched with oil, trying to desperately cover the bald spots. In contrast, his wife's silky hair was so black that it merged with the twilight. She was almost invisible, although her curious eyes followed the unexpected situation with interest.

Lázaro took a step forward, searching for a way to politely excuse himself and Lorenzo from the man's presence, but before he could open his mouth, Lorenzo walked stiffly around the room and sat down right in the middle of the table, between husband and wife, not daring to stare the patron in the eye. Lázaro was perplexed by the traveller's reaction, not really knowing what was going on. The boy knew that the only way out was finding Talita, so the dinner ritual could continue. That way, everyone could finish their fancy soups and get back to their own journeys. Lázaro's anxiety flared for a second at the thought of the future. *Where are our journeys taking us? Where is this stranger going?* He pushed the image of the End from his mind and answered the Mondragón. 'Yes my patron, I'll go help Ana Beatriz find the girl.' And Lázaro walked towards the set of stairs leading to the second floor, leaving Lorenzo alone.

Lázaro wandered through the long corridors, stopping to look inside each of the many rooms. Talita was small, so sometimes she hid in the most obscure places. After inspecting several with no luck, he saw some light spilling from underneath one of the doors. Lázaro approached and cautiously peered inside before entering; after all, the building was old, it could have been full of Animas. A whispered voice came from the room.

'Talita? Little girl, where are you? Talita? Are you inside the wardrobe?' Ana Beatriz stood in the middle of an empty

86

bedroom. Surrounding her was a small wardrobe, a humble bed and a window with heavy green curtains. It was her own room. The childminder approached the wardrobe, poised playfully.

'Let's see, let's see, I think I... found you!' She said as she flung open the wardrobe. A couple of white undergarments and a few working clothes hung in its austere interior, but no little girl was to be seen.

'You hid yourself somewhere different today, didn't you Talita? You wouldn't want the soup to go cold would you? Why don't you tell me where you are? Maybe... Under the bed!' Ana Beatriz threw herself to the floor, and peeked below the bed, lifting the hanging bedding from one side. Underneath it, nothing.

'Ha! I couldn't picture my little girl hiding under there, the dust would have ended up all over your beautiful new dress.' Talita's carer said as she brushed the dust off her own working clothes. She turned around and called for the girl again, this time approaching the window.

'Maybe you're hiding behind the curtains? That has always been your favourite hiding place, hasn't it? Let's see...' She wrenched the curtains apart. Again, nothing. Ana Beatriz closed the curtains, shut the wardrobe and arranged the bedding then she sighed and looked at the ceiling, defeated. She froze like this for a moment. She touched her face in desperation, wishing the day would finish already.

She must have worked so hard today, without my mother to give her a hand. Lázaro pitied her, when unexpectedly, her facial expression changed. Desperation was completely erased from her brain. The clock in her mind resetted with a mute click.

'Talita? Little girl, where are you? Talita? Are you inside the wardrobe?' Ana Beatriz stood in the middle of an empty bedroom. Surrounding her was a small wardrobe, a humble bed and a window with heavy green curtains. It was her own room. The childminder approached the wardrobe, poised playfully.

'Let's see, let's see, I think I... found you!' She said as she flung open the wardrobe. A couple of white undergarments and a few working clothes hung in its austere interior, but no little girl was to be seen. Lázaro observed her carefully, it was as if he was experiencing some form of manic deja-vu.

Again, Ana Beatriz repeated the same process; she looked under the bed, behind the curtains, reset everything to its original place, sighed, and started again.

'Talita? Little girl, where are you? Talita? Are you inside the wardrobe?' Lázaro stood outside the doorway and watched the curse at work. He could only wonder how many times she had repeated those very actions. She was stuck in a loop. After four whole repetitions, the boy decided on the best way to help the Portuguese childminder. Out of compassion, he entered the room.

'Ana Beatriz, the patron sent me to give you a hand. Where would you like me to look?' The woman jumped, scared at the interruption of her cursed ritual.

'Lázaro, *rapaz*, you really scared me! I feel like my heart is about to climb up my throat and escape my body. Yes, yes, *rapaz*, come find her with us. I think she may actually be hiding behind the curtains this time.' As the woman approached the curtains to unveil the nothing once again. Lázaro refused to be sucked into the senseless loop.

'Actually Ana Beatriz, I think I've heard Talita's voice coming out of that other room at the end of the corridor.

Maybe she's hiding somewhere in-'

'No, Lázaro.' The childminder interrupted the boy. 'She always, always, always hides in here. She must be here somewhere... Maybe inside the wardrobe!' She walked with purpose towards the wardrobe. Heartbroken, Lázaro couldn't take it anymore. He grabbed her from the wrist and pulled her out of the room into the corridor.

'Hey Ana, I think I can hear Talita over-' A smack rang out. Lázaro put his hand to his cheek. Ana Beatriz had slapped him so sharply that his face went numb for two whole seconds. And although Lázaro was not aware, the clocks ticked for those exact two seconds. The boy and the woman stared at each other in shared acknowledgement of the situation. In her eyes, Lázaro could see the real childminder awakening, but before she could break her pattern, she got lost inside the curse once again. She turned around and entered the room, sighed, and continued her search.

'You hid yourself somewhere different today, didn't you Talita? You wouldn't want the soup to go cold, would you? Why don't you tell me where you are?'

Lázaro gave up trying to save her. She was lost. *I cannot*

afford to join her in the curse, not today at least. Thought the boy as he carefully closed the door to Ana Beatriz's room, muttering a silent goodbye. The boy returned to the dining room, hoping that Lorenzo was still sane.

There, the young one found exactly what he had left. Lorenzo, sweating nervously, avoiding Lord Mondragón's stare over three plates of hot soup. Lord Mondragón's wife didn't say anything, and he predicted that she probably never would. Lázaro found it strange that someone who's ready to face the End by boldly travelling around the land, was so scared of the patron. The image of the slithering black horizon materialised ahead of him, almost calling him. He shook the image from his head and joined them in the silent banquet. He chose a seat opposite to Lorenzo, positioning them both between the patron and the lady of the house. She observed the whole situation in awe, they hadn't had guests for so long.

Lázaro thought desperately of an excuse to leave the palace; he wouldn't allow the only person he's seen unaffected by the curse be swallowed by it.

'Lorenzo... Lorenzo!' Lázaro whispered, trying to be discreet. The traveller was clearly ignoring the boy.

His anger bubbled up inside, more and more overtly signalling Lorenzo over the crockery. That was when the boy caught two little shoes poking out from the bottom of the curtains hanging behind the traveller. The boy, suddenly excited, ran over and pulled them open. The orange light of the sun flooded the room mercilessly. From their privileged location at the edge of the cliffs the tall windows revealed, in all its terrifying splendour, the thin line of despair rising in the horizon, approaching steadily from the West. It had advanced quite a way since the last time Lázaro looked. Lorenzo turned around, gazing with wide eyes out the window, astounded at the incoming evil.

'Talita, my daughter! I knew Lázaro could find you!' Exclaimed relieved Lord Mondragón.

'Yes Father! I am the best in the world at hide and seek!'

The patron and the girl laughed heartily. The mother of the girl, however, looked more interested in the boy. For a brief moment, she locked eyes with Lázaro; there was something different in the way she looked at him. He wondered if she was freed from the curse. She smiled eerily, as he tried to decipher the gesture.

Now it was the traveller who tried to get Lázaro's attention. Lorenzo pointed his head towards the exit. His discreet move grew progressively more evident until the boy noticed it. Understanding what the traveller meant, he nodded in reply. The moment between Lázaro and Lady Mondragón was gone. The guests knew that the more time they spent sitting there, the closer they would be to spending the eternity having soup; they stood up ready to leave. As they were about to do it, the patron interjected.

'Enough now! Everyone, take a seat. I command you.' The patron's rumbling voice made Lorenzo and Lázaro return promptly to their seats. 'Before we eat let's pray.' The Mondragón ordered, while grabbing Lorenzo's hand on one side, and Talita's on the other. Lady Mondragón reached out for Lázaro's hand; her touch was motherly and gentle. The traveller forgot about the rest of the world while holding the patron's hand; he had never met his father until that moment. Lorenzo closed his eyes, overwhelmed by emotion, letting the touch sink in. The grasped hands formed an unlikely circle around the dinner table.

As they closed their eyes and mumbled a prayer, both guests accepted their destiny, and sat comfortably in their seats for the rest of eternity.

That is what would have happened if Lady Mondragón hadn't released both their hands, while whispering 'Time to go, gentlemen. I'll take care of them. That's why god put me next to this man, after all.' Her crooked smile brought the boy back from the initial realms of the curse's nightmare. He opened his eyes. Lázaro, thanking the lady, quietly stood and crept away. Lorenzo followed, not without struggling from liberating his hand from the patron's grab. As they left the dining room, Lázaro understood that the soup would remain served on the table forever.

Or at least until the End reached the palace.

V - THE CONVERSATION

In which Lorenzo decides to lie; and Lázaro decides to have hope.

The heavy wooden doors to the back garden slammed open as Lorenzo rushed out from the palace. He was breathing for the first time since the boy opened the curtains. Since the boy had revealed the dooming landscape from the dining room's window. Fresh air filled his lungs. The traveller was in shock, and wanted nothing more than to get out of the suffocating palace's grounds as soon as possible. Lázaro couldn't understand the stranger's behaviour, but felt relieved that they had avoided the danger of allowing the curse into their hearts. Stuck forever in a prayer, playing hide and seek, or eating a soup that will never cool down. The pair had no idea for how long they stayed inside the palace, but Lázaro guessed it must have been longer than it seemed. The End had consumed most of the mountains on the horizon. The threatening line merged with the Sun; its lower half lost to oblivion.

The back gardens hung at the edge of the cliff, its boundaries marked by a white marble bannister that crowned the abyss in front of them. Tropical trees mixed with Ronda's original flora, watered by white marble channels carved into the soil. They spread across the ground, decorated with colourful mosaics and filled with water that, in the past, had been flowing freely. A garden to compete with paradise. Lorenzo moved towards the bannister, facing away from Lázaro so the boy could not see the tears that ran down his face. He leaned heavily against the barrier, feeling the sun against his skin. The traveller now knew that every attempt of fleeing would be met with the End, for they were surrounded by it.

'What on Earth were you thinking?' The boy piped up angrily. As soon as the question had left his mouth, he remembered the many times his own mother had used those words towards him. Probably in that very spot, after he had played a devilish prank on one of the garden cats, or cut some exotic flowers to give away to a child in the square. Now Lázaro's mother was asleep, with a temperature, waiting for the End to embrace her like the rest of Ronda were doing. 'Soon mum, very soon,' the boy mumbled to himself, joining Lorenzo by the bannister.

Lorenzo had nothing else to lose. He had made it to the palace. He had met the patron, a man he had met many times before in his imagination. He took a deep breath and got ready to pronounce out loud the scariest of sentences. 'That man, your patron, is my father.'

It took Lázaro a moment to understand what the stranger was saying. *The patron has only one daughter, what does he mean?* Thought the boy as he waited for the stranger to continue.

'My mother was the maid before your mother, Adelaida was her name. Did your mother ever mention... Nah probably not, my mother was like a sigh, very quiet, but she could make your problems disappear with just her presence. Your 'patron' loved that, or so I've heard. I mean, I didn't know who he was until recently, she never talked too much about him. It was my grandma who told me when-' Lorenzo stopped one second to swallow the fact that his grandma wasn't in this world anymore. 'Apparently he always provided for my family, even from far away. I just needed to meet him before... everything disappears.' The traveller was breathing deeply, fighting back his tears from pouring in front of the boy.

Lázaro was outraged by this unveiled secret. The Mondragón were the role models of the whole of Ronda, this news didn't match with his idea of the patron at all. *How many other secrets may be hidden within the walls of the palace; within the bedrock of Ronda.* Lázaro wondered in silence, understanding very well the pain of the traveller, for them both were fatherless now.

'Let's go back inside, Lorenzo!' Lázaro's rage spoke. 'You need to confront him and make sure he knows what he did to you. To your mother!'

'No, kid. My mother's story ended years ago, there's no way of closing it down differently. She got ill when I was your age, and slowly withered. She died surrounded by everyone who loved her- but before she left...' Lorenzo couldn't contain the tears anymore. 'She made me promise I wouldn't keep one ounce of hatred in my heart.' They stood side by side and both thought about their mothers. Lázaro had never felt more connected to anyone, both hearts breaking at the same pace, like gigantic glaciers cracking and melting into the ocean. The pair silently reflected on the similarity and difference in their lives. Two sides of the same coin.

Lázaro was still trying to make sense of this revelation. *It would have definitely been a scandal back in its day. María, Perpetua and Eustaquia would have enough conversation for another eternity,* the boy smiled at the thought. As they faced the End from atop the balcony, they did not notice a gentle breeze rocking the palm trees, crown to leaflet.

Not only has this man crossed the Sierra in the twilight, but he has also left his town to find his father! This traveller is everything I should have been. I will follow him forever, and hopefully I'll grow to become as brave as he is. Lázaro's mind wandered while his eyes followed the undulating movements of the ominous horizon.

I am a coward. I ran away until I had nowhere else to hide. I couldn't even tell my father who I am and now I'm crying in front of a kid. Well done Lorenzo. What are you gonna do now? The End is everywhere... Ronda may as well be the last remaining town on Earth. Lorenzo was frozen, not a glimpse of courage to be found within himself. It would be only a matter of time for the curse to claim his soul.

'The End is getting way closer now. Look, there's no mountains between here and there anymore...' The mention of it brought Lorenzo back from his fears to the paradisiacal garden. The traveller was lost for words, he did not know what to do anymore, so he remained in silence. Lázaro, however, was getting excited, he was going to take action just like the stranger was. He would become another traveller, so that they could journey together in fellowship. From where they were standing, they could see the pharaonic walls of the palace merging with the rocky cliff. Through the gaping window presiding over the fall, Lorenzo discerned his own father praying. The stranger nodded a sad farewell towards the cursed family.

'See you in another life, old man.' He muttered under his breath while turning around, leaving the cliffs and Lázaro behind. He didn't know where he was going, but his fear apparently did. He walked decidedly to the exit.

'Lorenzo, please-' Lázaro watched as the traveller left him behind. Like his father did. *If he leaves I will be all by myself again, waiting for the End, no better than a rock in this cliff. If I go, I will have to leave behind everyone I know.*

My mother... If there's a chance to understand this curse, experience new things, meet other brave people- I will have to join the traveller, for Ronda's sake, and my own. A bit of wind rushed around the garden, disturbing the slumbering green, urging the boy to run after Lorenzo. He ran.

He quickly overtook the traveller and reached the garden door before he did, slamming it shut. 'Where are you going now? You are leaving Ronda, right?' Lázaro enquired as Lorenzo's fears unleashed inside his belly. Lázaro misinterpreted the traveller's horrified expression as an affirmation. 'I knew it! Take me with you please! I will rot and die in cowardice and stillness if I don't leave! Please Lorenzo, you are the bravest human left on Earth... Take me with you. Give me a chance to bring change to the world.'

I am a coward, however this awakened boy thinks I'm filled with a fire capable of replacing the sun. I am empty inside, prepared for the curse, ready to wait. Why does Lázaro remind me of myself before I lost all hope? Thought the traveller, as pins and needles covered his legs. Fear, and the curse, had receded. Lorenzo looked at Lázaro, seeing only a boy who wanted a friend for the end of the world. *What evil could bear entertaining a boy for a bit until the curse gets to both of us? Hopefully we won't feel anything by the time we meet the dark nothingness.* The idea of waiting in company soothed Lorenzo's anxiety, however, he wasn't ready to admit that to himself.

A moment of anticipation, and then an answer.

'Yes, I will let you join me, Lazarillo. Just let's be on our way, we may not have as long as we think.' Lorenzo gave in, surprising even himself. Lázaro, not being able to contain his joy, celebrated to himself effusively pacing around the stranger. *At last! I'm having fun again! I'm not alone anymore!*

They were about to commence their adventure outside of Ronda when a question interrupted his celebration. *Every adventurer needs a goal, a quest.* The boy did not know what kind of journey he was signing in for, not that it would have made him change his mind.

'And, where are we going, Lorenzo?'

'You know what? I will let you pick that one. What's to see around here?' The traveller asked back to Lázaro, not being able to think of a good answer that would, hopefully, take them as far from the edges of the End as possible.

'I know! Let me take you to my favourite place. It's towards the End's direction but maybe, if we get closer, we will be able to take a good look at it... Just follow me!' Exclaimed Lázaro, thrilled.

Lorenzo however had already started to regret his decision, as he turned his head to have a quick look at the threatening horizon. He didn't know it yet, but this adventure would lead them straight into the End's fauces.

VI - THE WITCH

In which they speak to the trees; leave their bodies; then hold hands.

The trail Lázaro used to reach the ruined mill was almost invisible to the untrained eye. As they left Ronda behind, the overgrown firs and cork oaks became more dense around them, receiving the pair into their domain. The orange light of the sun forced its way through the tangled green limbs that netted and crawled above them. The branches wrestled, in absolute stillness, over which would be the ones to absorb the day's last drops of light. Their labyrinthic poses shielded the pair from the frozen sky. As the odd fellowship began their new adventure, a silent truth was suggested in everything they laid eyes upon; the rocks waited, so did the trees, so did the soil. In fact, they all had been waiting since the dawn of time, and only now was it so apparent. Lázaro and Lorenzo were walking at a good pace, when a hum assaulted their ears - a growing yawn, waking up, picking up speed. It did not come from the air around them, it was a vibration that came from the ground, that grew like a plant. Breaking through the soil, and piercing through the soles of their feet. It entered them. They stopped walking and looked at each other, trying to understand if they were imagining it or it was a shared experience. The muted sound resonated in their bones and muscles, invading their whole body. They could not avoid listening to it, listening to a strange call for help as they covered their ears with their hands in vain. Lázaro understood that their only way out of the physical struggle was to give in, to surrender their bodies. He opened all of his doors to the call.

The relief was automatic, although the hum was still there, now it was nothing but a background sound that cushioned the scene. The boy felt as if he was floating, and upon a second inspection of this feeling, he realised the reason. He was seeing himself from above, he had abandoned his body and he was now hovering over it, at a maintained distance. In his new formless existence, his every move required his complete focus. Trying to move his head and open his mouth to shout a warning was pointless, for he had no mouth, no head and no legs anymore. Only his thoughts were left. He was his thoughts, nothing else. *Lorenzo! Are we dead? Are we dying? Save yourself! Run away!* The traveller didn't hear the boy's appeal. He had also removed his hands from his ears, his body had stopped struggling against the hum. It was clear to the boy that he had also invited the sound to take over.

In frustrated silence, Lázaro observed from above how his body twitched, as it slowly commenced to walk. The movement was very slow, as if whatever that was controlling their bodies was getting accustomed to the new limbs. Lorenzo's body followed, as they slowly abandoned the well known path, and advanced into the depths of the forest. Lorenzo's thoughts joined Lázaro's in the air above them.

'Boy, where are you going! I'm here! What is happening to me?'

'Lorenzo? Can you hear me?'

'Yes! Please slap me or something. I must be dreaming. Take me back, down to the ground!'

'I can't, I am not myself either. I am not sure there's much we can do other than watch.'

And so they witnessed their own figures as they walked past bushes and trees, past ponds and nettles. They moved so slow that they walked for an eternity, not really knowing if their consciousness would ever return to themselves.

'No, no, no. I knew we should have never left Ronda.'

'What do you mean, traveller? This was your idea.'

Lorenzo realised that in this new form, he had to be careful with his thoughts. *{I need to keep them to myself, otherwise he will see right through my cowardice}*. He put some effort on protecting the private information, hugging it with the arms of the mind.

Channelling a new string of ideas towards Lázaro, he prepared himself to answer the accusatory question.

'Yes, but-'

'This must be a dream, I've had one like this before. A weird one, right before you arrived.'

'It makes sense to think that we fell asleep.'

'Or maybe we are dead, and this is heaven?'

'Or maybe we are dead, and this is hell.' Lorenzo added, observing how the foliage around them turned into stranger shapes and silhouettes of fear. *{Has this boy dragged me*

straight into the End? Is this how my nan felt when she went through?} Wondered Lorenzo, watching from above, as he panically tried to order his body to run away. His body did not respond, the hum was calling.

'What is being alive, anyway?' Lorenzo's consciousness slipped as it was about to get lost in the endless pondering of human existence. A sudden movement caught his full attention. Whoever was controlling their bodies had heard his existential question, and was using their new eyes to stare right through where Lorenzo's consciousness was suspended in the air. They could hear the pair's floating thoughts, and they expected Lorenzo to answer his own difficult question.

Terrified, the traveller felt exposed, ashamed and embarrassed while holding the scrutinising stare. He felt like an imposter, a dumb excuse for a knight in shining armour.

{'I'm a pariah'}.

'What is being alive, anyway?' Lázaro thought as well, infected by the venomous nature of Lorenzo's open ended question. He repeated it over and over to the vast

emptiness around him, like an echo in an eternal cave, rebounding forever. They were losing their minds without fleshy boundaries to contain them, without their senses to navigate the world. The two bodies stopped staring at their thinking counterparts and returned to their walking. As the growth became denser, they started to push themselves through impossible spaces. Their clothes got covered in the sap that emanated from the thick trees, and the sticky liquid created long thin threads that marked their lethargic advances.

'Lázaro! Are you there? I'm scared.'

'I'm here. I'm here.'

'Lázaro, don't leave me, please. I need you with me.'

After having spent so long by himself, those words meant everything to the boy. Having someone to share this adventure with made his heart feel fuzzy; an arrangement of warm glints burst somewhere inside his chest. Hope shone so bright that they could see it like a brooch in their chests, from their vantage point.

'What is that light, boy?'

'I am not sure, but it feels good.'

'It does. It feels like home. Is it coming from-'

'Yes, it's coming from inside me. I think it's there because of you, you know? I think you've inspired me with your spirit.'

Lorenzo wasn't sure how to answer that statement. He couldn't have inspired anyone to do anything. He thought himself worthless, after all. Lázaro, encouraged by his inner light, felt like talking about something forbidden.

'What are you going to do when the dark horizon reaches us?'

Lorenzo took his time to answer, measuring his words carefully, controlling the need to scream; making sure there was no trace of desperation in his tone.

'I don't know, I think I'll try and talk to it.' Lorenzo said eventually, trying to dodge the subject.

'Talk to it? Do you think you can talk to that monster?' Lázaro was amazed by the bravery of the traveller; his words dispelled any trace of fear inside the boy. {Talk to the End!? This person is tougher than all my father's men, and half the size than any of them}.

'Yes, I don't know, why wouldn't you. Maybe it's just a case of asking politely to stop devouring everything we know. You *never know with these things.'* Lorenzo reasoned out loud, feeling stupid for saying such a senseless thing. *{Well done Lorenzo, now you sound like a complete fool. Talk to the End!? As if it was a misbehaving child!}*

Lázaro, however, was bewildered. This crazy travelling man had the guts to stop right in front of the very End of things and demand it to stop. It was that place and moment when Lázaro decided- *{If I am ever given the chance to grow up, I would want to become as brave as Lorenzo}*. Lázaro was in the middle of picking his next question, out of the plethora of them that filled his mind to its very brim. Luckily for the traveller, something else got in the way of their bodies.

Lonely in the depths of the forest, there was an olive branch. And on top of the branch, a single flame danced endlessly. Not spreading but burning in the very same spot, never progressing in its labour. No smoke, no smell, just a bright tongue of blue fire performing for them.

'Will o' the wisp!' Gasped Lorenzo as they both saw their bodies approaching the flame. Shadows swayed at the light of the wisp, stretching over each other.

'This dream feels too real, perhaps we are awake, after all.'

'How did this fire start? How is it even burning?'

Their bodies kneeled next to the flame, and turned around their heads to look at their hanging consciousnesses. As slowly as a flower blooms, those who controlled their bodies extended their arms, then opened their right hand, and without hesitation tried to grab the blue flame. Lázaro and Lorenzo observed in horror as their bodies were being burnt in front of them.

'Stop what you are doing! You are going to hurt us!' Pleaded Lorenzo to his own reflection, who looked at him intently, trying to convey a message.

The searing pain didn't make them wait. Even away from their bodies, they felt their hands burn with their whole being. Their hands pulsed under the punishment of the blue flame. They were feeling every single crease of their hand bubbling and bursting, cracking and cooking under the relentless heat. The nails and the dirt under them melted and mixed at the touch of the blue spell.

{'Thinking a scream is not as effective'}. Realised Lázaro, enveloped by the fire, as he quickly took his hand away from the heat, falling on his back. He could not stop hissing and looking at his palm, assessing the damage caused by the stray flame. Not a single sign of burning remained in his olive skin, not even a small trace of harm. He looked across the flame to find that Lorenzo was as surprised as he was. Both looked at their hands in awe, as they realised they were back inside their own bodies. The pain was the trigger, they were back in control.

They took a second lying on their backs, staring at the immobile tree branches above them. The trees were higher in that part of the forest, a part so remote that the boy had never been there, and everything around them was now presented as unremarkably normal. Everything but the blue will o'wisp.

'After seeing the world with the eye of the mind, reality seems a bit plain' Spoke the boy inside his head, expecting Lorenzo to hear him. No response; they were not connected anymore.

'Lázaro, can you hear me? Are you ok?'

'Yes, I'm here. That was-'

'Were we- Were you floating above our heads?'

'I was. We were? Together?'

'We must have fallen asleep, that was all. If we think too much about it we'll go crazy before we can get out of this place. Let's get up and keep on walking, I don't know where we are and the End must be getting dangerously closer.' He spoke as he stood up, dusted his traveller's garments and avoided acknowledging the wicked blue fire. 'Let's go, boy. Follow my lead'.

With fear as fuel, the man pretended bravery as an excuse for his prompt exit. He did not care about getting lost in the deep forest, he just wanted to get out of there, fast. Lázaro stood again, still not fully in control of his legs, trying to keep up with Lorenzo's newfound pace. Rushing down a random path, Lorenzo left the flame dancing on its own.

'Oh boy, I do hope we never see any other weird stuff like that. I'm done'.

'But Lorenzo, we're cursed. Everything is weird now.'

'Yeah but did you see how our hands melted in that little fire? Did you feel it? Not something I would like to repeat. Thank you kindly but nope, thanks!' He walked with big steps as Lázaro tried to follow closely. The traveller halted his hike abruptly, and the boy bumped into him.

In front of them, two blue flames of similar sizes had appeared. Lorenzo took a finger to his lips, asking his fellow adventurer to stay put put in total silence. Looking around, nothing moved but the wisps. They felt like it was their very first time discovering fire. Without any notice, and further down the place where they stood, another flame, a bit bigger this time, ignited. The light beckoned them. A clear call for adventure. A mystery to solve.

'I think we need to follow them, Lorenzo.'

'My grandma used to tell me that the will o' the wisps were like love; if you follow them, they run away... But if you run away, they will hunt you until your very end,' Lorenzo said, letting his voice tremble, not masking his true feelings.

How honourable of you, Lorenzo, to feel sad when talking about your grandma, thought Lázaro as he felt his inner furnace of hope getting warmer. They were about to enter a new side of the forest, an area that had been untouched for millennia, until the curse graced the land. 'Your grandma was a wise woman, Lorenzo. I think we have no choice but to follow them if we want to get out of this part of the forest.'

The traveller nodded, as he promised himself to stay as far away as possible from anything that could cause him a serious burn.

They ventured deeper into the forest, as the tiny flames kept revealing themselves everywhere. Some sat at the union of the ground and a tree's bark, while others climbed the branches above their heads or hid below the protruding roots around them. The path kept on descending, as Lázaro led the expedition route marked by the titling lights. Lorenzo was about to trip a couple times, so he grabbed Lázaro's shoulder to find support. The boy felt happy to be useful to the traveller in his journey, so he kept pushing through the undergrowth, smiling. The fire observed them as they walked deeper, towards the witch.

The blue fire continued to expand as they progressed their journey, swallowing whole trees around them and slowly increasing the temperature of the woods. The boy was breaking a sweat, as they continued to explore the green realm. Occasional burning trees quickly became rows of them, no crepitations anywhere to be heard, as if sound had been swallowed by the curse. However there was a new noise that rose from the trees - a dim whisper built from many voices. The trees were talking to them. A quiet hum. Lázaro didn't speak their language, but he understood.

'Keep walking Lorenzo, they need us.'

'Is that the same hum from before? Was it them, the trees, who took over our bodies?'

'I think so my friend, it will be ok now. They are too weak. They just want us to continue to walk. Trees are nature, they must be friendly...'

Lorenzo didn't ask how the boy knew what the hum meant, so he followed his lead, as the blue light and the heat became the only thing around them. Green gave way to a blue tint that covered their clothes and faces. The whole forest was burning.

Lázaro really wanted to shield his eyes from the blinding brightness, but he knew he had to follow the whispers. The trees continued to call for help, silently witnessing the strangers as they progressed through the path, as they were consumed in pain. Behind them the fire was slowly closing, spreading in silence and threatening to devour them as much as it was ravaging the surrounding scenery. They could only walk forward, there was no return.

Swallowed by a tunnel of raging flames, the heat was almost unbearable. Lorenzo remembered the vision of his melting hand, and searched Lázaro's for protection. They held hands under the parade of destruction. The tunnel closed above them. The pair of adventurers did not protest as they fell victim to the azure storm, as they walked through the corridor of pure fire. They looked at each other, knowing that they had to reach the end of it or perish trying. The mourning silence around them broke as the trees started to give in. They had held the safe passage all they could, now it was time for them to allow the fire to finish the job. A crack, then a hollow thump, then a thousand creaks - the tunnel started to crumble all over them.

Waking from the surreal daydream, Lorenzo, keeping Lázaro's hand tight, pulled from the boy and started to run towards the exit. The debris and dust flew all around them, they could not see where they were going. And then they fell.

Cooler air embraced their bodies, making them shiver. No

noise, no smell, no smoke. The trees were far behind them, as they could see the fire spreading deeper into the forest. They had reached the safety of a forest clearing, from which the streets and houses of Ronda became almost visible. Recovering from the fall, Lorenzo helped Lázaro up, as they tried to figure out their location. A hill rose immediately next to them.

'Let's climb that hill Lorenzo, I'll be able to tell in which direction to walk so we can get out of here'.

The traveller nodded. They squinted their eyes tightly as they climbed the hill, trying to recover from the abrasive experience they had just suffered. After their eyes had adapted to the amount of light, they found themselves in a higher point over the raging treetops. Everything was visible from the elevated ground; the forest being consumed, the whole city of Ronda, the sun, and the End itself. The cliffs of Ronda seemed to be a silent prayer adorned by a town devoid of genuine life. The cliffs prayed for the End to turn around.

At the very top of the hill where they stood, there was a sturdy but delicate bonfire, releasing a smoke plume that

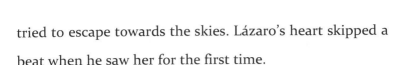

tried to escape towards the skies. Lázaro's heart skipped a beat when he saw her for the first time.

A naked woman danced manically around the bonfire, to the silence of the burning woods. Her long, black, wet hair moved around her, with delayed reaction to her actions, as if each strand had a spirit of its own. She pranced around, jumping incredibly high, pointing at the fire and repeating complex hand gestures. The witch seemed to be signalling the fire to act upon her commands and as she did, the blue expanded over the green all around them. But the boy was not fooled. The witch spell was one against the curse, a spell to bring back time, Lázaro understood. Her nakedness hid a secret meaning, a requirement of her ritual, an ingredient to the witch's plan. Lorenzo and Lázaro froze, witnessing without knowing it a ritual of fire that had been performed since the origins of humanity. In the bonfire, the dark pillar of smoke was struggling to form. Following her every command, the fire challenged the absence of time and elevated in response to the long nailed, bony fingers of the pagan conductor. Slowly, a dense cloud of black smoke emerged.

Lázaro wanted to run away, fearing he was too close to one of the boy-devouring witch Eustaquia and Perpetua had described a million times before that moment. He had been scared of witches for as long as he could remember. Lorenzo observed the frantic hand movements, and started to pick up certain sounds coming out from the witches mouth.

'A witch,' the traveller mumbled, confirming the kid's worst fears. Lázaro tightened his hand around Lorenzo's. The traveller responded by also tightening his grip.

The woman kept dancing. Her silhouette twisted against the dying sun. Lázaro closed his eyes, trying to gather some strength to confront the inevitable encounter. The higher the smoke column spiralled, the quicker the woman danced. The witch started to emit sounds that reminded them of wild animals, two different noises from the same throat. The burning trees screamed in agony, and they did it so furiously that their voices reached the pair. The whispers had become an overwhelming plea that crawled all the way to their ears, and introduced themselves into their bodies. They felt the hum taking over once again, but

123

this time, only the muscles around their neck obeyed. Their heads turned to face the forest. In the middle of the blue pandemonium, the crowns cried while being consumed by the witch's spell. All trees were slowly dying but one - a gigantic white fig stood firm in the middle of the forest, completely shattered as it observed the destruction of their kind. As soon as their eyes rested on the white bark of the skyscraping tree, the hum became an old voice. The voice of a tree that had witnessed the land of Ronda from its very beginning. A voice they heard with their minds - slow, a glitch, a long sigh.

You should be the sacrifice. We were here before you. You should be the ones to burn.

Lorenzo's face contorted in panic, trying to escape the control of the tree's voices. But his efforts to release himself were futile, he started to turn around and face the bonfire. His feet slowly directed his body into the big pile of smoke and embers. The witch continued in a trance, developing the fire ritual towards its chaotic conclusion.

Lázaro couldn't move at all. He only observed Lorenzo as he walked in the direction of the fire. His hands were still together.

Lorenzo! I will not let you go!

Boy, help me, I don't want to burn.

Focus on my hand. Keep it tight around mine.

The bonfire growled and a stream of smoke, as black as the horizon, emerged from the embers and spiralled towards the sky. The witch laughed, and the two witnesses knew, without communicating with each other, that the ceremony was close to its completion. The witch was bringing time back.

The trees controlling Lorenzo abandoned their gentle movements and turned aggressive and violent. His body was a knot of spasms and jumps, as he forcibly tried to release the body from Lázaro's grip.

I'm not going to let you go! I won't!

But the trees were many, and the trees were ancient. The boy's hand gave up and Lorenzo's body was free to burn. The legs of the traveller struggled to follow the straight path ahead of him; after all, trees don't have any use for them. Controlling his limbs, they tried to get him closer to the witch. *You will be the one to be sacrificed*, they said.

Lorenzo's legs tried in vain to sustain the man's weight and direct him to the bonfire. Trying to move bones and flesh as if they were branching knots and sap, the trees tangled the traveller's legs, who tripped and fell to the ground.

Lost in her spell, the witch failed to see the fallen man. Her bony legs crumbled at the obstacle, joining him on the floor. She opened her eyes, awaken. The trance had finished too early. The ritual unfinished, the circle broken. The bonfire's heat dissipated in a blink of an eye, burning cold. The smoke pillar froze against the sky. The blue fire consuming the trees froze. The white fig remained untouched as it observed the End approach. The spell was gone, and the trees would be frozen in pain until the End spared them.

The witch jumped back into all fours, hissed and stared at the pair, deeply, as if into their souls. Full of timeless hate and frustration, her body convulsed and started to run into the ignited forest, screaming curses in a language that wasn't created for the pair's ears. The witch retreated away from the horizon and made her way to the cliffs of Ronda. Lorenzo stared at the retreating woman, secretly thanking her for stopping the trees from controlling his body. Slowly, they regained control over their limbs and recovered from the traumatic experience. All the pain of the ritual disappeared with the witch. Her attempt to bring back time and stop the curse, hijacked by nature's arrogance.

'Lorenzo! Are you ok my friend?' Asked the boy as he kneeled next to his fallen companion. 'I think the trees are frozen now. They won't be a problem anymore. I cannot hear them.'

'Neither can I. That was horrible. I thought I was done.'

'I am sorry I let your hand go.'

'It's ok, it was the trees who released your grip. I am sure of it.'

They looked at the frozen forest, feeling the curse fill all the space around them.

'I won't be able to look at trees under the same light ever again.' Lorenzo complained as he rubbed his wrist. And Lázaro chuckled.

'Look at the horizon. I think there's still time before the End arrives.'

'What do you mean, boy?'

'I want you to see my favourite place before it disappears from our world,' reiterated Lázaro, candidly 'I wouldn't want you to stop this adventure just because of some mean spirited branches who want to see you burn!' he continued, as Lorenzo digested his words. They were free from the green curse within the curse.

Lorenzo looked to the black line of the End, that continued to crawl defiantly. It seemed to sneer at them, celebrating that the witch was not strong enough to stop it. Celebrating that the realm of the living had lost its last option for salvation. Lázaro thought he heard something again, while looking at the terrible final boundary. It seemed to whisper like the trees did, only faintly.

Nothing finishes without me.

Lorenzo realised that Lázaro had ushered them straight into the End's trajectory. As fear returned back into the traveller's chest, he snapped out of his dream-like state, standing up, leaving the boy's side. Lázaro felt completely alone - his inner brooch of light quickly dimming. They had been holding their hands so tightly. Even after they let go of each other during the ritual, their hands continued to feel the pressure around them, just as if they were still being held. The curse perpetuated their touch forever, in a world without time.

VII - THE RUINED MILL

In which Lázaro changes destinations; Lorenzo climbs a tower; and the curse devours a heart.

Lázaro and Lorenzo could barely see the frozen fumes or the burning patch of woodlands anymore. In front of them, on the forgotten path, a row of ancient, dilapidated mills followed the curve of the river. The occasional derelict building sat next to an army of suspicious looking olive trees. None of this fazed Lázaro, who was back on the familiar route he knew by heart, leading to his favourite place. Their minds felt as if a cloud was embracing them. The muttering trees, the tall smoke and the wild witch - it all seemed a far away dream. A dream that could have visited them the previous night or a night years ago, neither of them could remember *when* it happened.

Was that the passing of time I felt? pondered Lázaro, distracted, as he scanned his body; embracing the brand new feeling in his chest.

The traveller was starting to doubt if the encounter with the woman had actually taken place, as they moved further away from the raging forest, further away from the spell to bring back time. Or perhaps his mind had other terrible thoughts to prioritise - whatever dangers laid ahead of the path that Lázaro had chosen.

They both walked at the same pace, sharing the foretelling silence. They both saw the advancing nothingness.

There was something Lázaro could no longer ignore, for as the woodland burnt and the lady danced, a spark in his heart had caught fire. The boy was now ignited from the inside, and he now knew what this brooch of light meant. As he felt the warmth he was radiating, the young one closed his eyes, feeling an overwhelming passion pushing every single corner of his body, almost reviving his cold and frozen carcass. *Does Lorenzo feel this, too?* the boy wondered, not gathering enough bravery to ask. He knew Lorenzo would leave him soon, and he wouldn't be able to follow. The boy did not have much time left to think of a plan. He had to keep the traveller around for as long as he could; at least until they could have a look at the End. Lázaro continued plotting during the trek to his favourite ruined mill, while expecting to be sent back to Ronda at any second. Forcing himself to focus solely in the warmth inside his chest, he decided to interpret its presence as a sign of the righteousness of his actions.

Lorenzo continued his walk in silence. He felt no passion, instead he felt crippling anxiety, turning everything around him dull and empty; *is the curse finally claiming my heart for good?* He feared, while following the path mindlessly. The boy looked at him often, making the traveller even more nervous. *I knew the plan was to entertain the kid, but things are only getting weirder and weirder. Plus he's taking me in the End's direction - I need to figure out how to get rid of him and hide somewhere in Ronda before the final hour.* Lázaro looked at him once more, trying to solve Lorenzo's puzzled face. 'I still can't believe I've found a true adventurer to explore the world with! Aren't you excited? If we're lucky you may even have that little chat with the End!' The boy's passion turned into fireworks in his belly as he talked about more adventures. An idea brewed in his mind.

Lorenzo caught a glimpse of hope when he started to feel something inside his chest. On a second thought, he realised that what he felt were palpitations. No magical brooch of hope left for him. *I am just a coward, after all.*

'I just don't think-' the traveller commenced before a knot in his throat blocked any sound. He started breathing heavily. He was older. He had seen more, and he knew the nature of life. He knew there were no happy endings; that life rarely waits for you to tell your whole story.

The boy stopped walking and stared at him, awaiting orders like a newly trained puppy. Lorenzo looked the kid in the eye, trying to be open about his overwhelming fear. Lázaro looked at him with starry eyes, awaiting for the traveller's wisdom.

The traveller was overcome with sorrow at the thought of breaking the boy's hopeful heart. He took a deep breath and spoke. 'I just don't think we should get too close to the End, I am concerned for your safety. This is after all your very first adventure. Let's see this place you talk about and then we can run in the opposite direction to find new and safer adventures. Right?' The traveller sighed relieved, *this excuse should do the trick,* he wrongly thought.

Lázaro was over the moon at the thought of more

adventures. 'Yes, you're right. Let's reach the ruined mill quickly and then we can be off to find a new horizon to explore!' The boy resumed the march through the forest, stepping surely and walking faster than before. *He's gonna keep me with him for his travels! We are free from the curse! At last, we are alive! Just a bit closer to the End and we'll have a clear view of it,* celebrated Lázaro wearing the widest smile in his rosy cheeked face, knowing that he was pushing his luck, secretly ushering the traveller closer to the End. *If I could only look at it from a bit closer, I would probably understand everything a bit better.* And just like that, out of sheer curiosity, this adventure's main goal shifted for the boy. They had to get closer, past the ruined mill. They had to see it up close.

They had to understand.

Lorenzo rolled his eyes as he continued to follow Lázaro, unknowingly, towards the End.

Rows of olive trees yielded to another patch of forest. They kept walking in silence; lost in their thoughts.

It wasn't long until they reached one of the abandoned mills, sitting in the middle of a clearing, appearing almost intact. The river drew a clear path around it, filtered by a bed of beautiful black rocks that had been forcefully polished by the waters. Everything stuck in time, as if they were part of a vivid masterpiece by the most talented painter that ever existed. The big water wheel remained in complete stillness. Foam adorned the water and rocktops, the leaves and woods stuck in the frenzy action, all of them cursed in water frozen in time. They walked through the structure, discovering its fragility in the supports of the roof. The tiles from one side had completely fallen, covering the floor with red dust. The other half stayed in perfect equilibrium over the wooden beams, waiting for time to reappear so they could crash against the floor. Lorenzo and Lázaro observed as the traveller racked his brains for something to say. *We cannot continue on this path, we have to go back to Ronda.* The traveller stopped walking, staring at the painted-like land around them, taking in the surprising fact that the curse could bring beauty into the world. The river was visible from one of the openings in the wall, so he sat and stared at the halted river, not knowing what to do. Fear was clawing his heart, stronger than ever. Lorenzo went pale, finding it difficult to breathe. *I cannot let him see that I'm dying of fear, I'm the older one! Shame on your cowardice Lorenzo!*

'It's not this one,' Lázaro beckoned Lorenzo, 'my favourite is the next one along the river, just a little bit further down the path. You're gonna love it, it's almost completely destroyed but it's got the prettiest baby Jesus statue you'd ever seen...' the boy stopped, Lorenzo was sitting down and clearly not paying attention. *I have to think of something quickly to keep him walking, we are so close to it!*

'Ok boy, that sounds cool-' Lorenzo pointed out, coldly 'I like this mill, it feels safe. And we can see the river. It's actually quite easy to imagine it flowing again, on its way to the End.' Shivers ran down his body imagining the water rushing towards the endless fall. *Is that what lies after the horizon? Will we fall forever?* Lorenzo tried to regain composure and continued, 'If I close my eyes I can even hear the echo of the water rushing, opening its way through the land and-'

'Yes, but you should really see the next one, honestly, it's better in every single way!' Lázaro was running out of excuses, his ulterior motive being exposed, *I need to buy myself some time. I want nothing more than to confront whatever lies ahead with Lorenzo.*

The traveller knew it was now or never.

'Lázaro please, let's sit by the river and talk.'

The boy knew it was now or never.

Lázaro seized the opportunity to speak. He blurted the first thought that came to mind 'Yes Lorenzo, I wanted to talk to you as well. I have been thinking as we were walking down here, and I have a theory. Listen please, this could change everything!' Lorenzo took his hands and covered his face with them, completely done with the boy's attempts at pretending that there was any hope for either of them. 'You know that I am the son of the servants of the Mondragón family, right?' Lorenzo tried to interject, but the boy was unstoppable '-and- my dad is one of his most valued workers, therefore I would, without a doubt, end up becoming one of his workers... As soon as I am of age... And I could potentially get better at it than my dad.

And my dad is really *really* good.' Lázaro walked in circles next to Lorenzo as he spoke. The information came out of his mouth messy and scrambled, producing an incipient headache on the tense traveller, who could not find any opportunity to respond. The boy paused, he was aware he hadn't said what he truly wanted to say.

'Are you following me Lorenzo?' Lázaro asked the despairing stranger, who didn't reply. 'What I'm trying to say here is that I am a servant of the Mondragón myself. And that means technically I am a servant of yourself, as you are a Mondragón by birth. So please, accept my offer in aiding you on your quests. And I promise we will have plenty of those quests, in the opposite direction of the End... Way past Ronda and the rest of the region. I know we should avoid the End, but how can we avoid something we don't know much about? If we get close enough we may learn something valuable, something important! We could even stop it!'

Silence hung thick in the air.

'Please?' The boy insisted, 'we can't run away for the rest of our lives.' He stared at the traveller with resolve.

Lorenzo held his breath, he could feel all the bottled up emotions force their way to the surface, the same emotions he had to swallow down when he had looked out from the Mondragón's window. He began to cry. The boy wasn't expecting it. He approached him carefully and put a hand on his back, in a confused attempt to comfort him. They stood there for a while, but the fire inside Lázaro was still blazing. So he kept talking.

'You came here bringing all this light and power into my life, making time feel like it was flowing again.' Lorenzo could not look at the boy, the shame was too much. 'And thinking about it, we actually made things change around us: the Mondragón found Talita, that weird witch got to set the forest on fire, you stopped me from jum-' Lázaro couldn't believe he almost confessed his cowardice. He reworded his thoughts and went straight to the point. 'What I'm saying is that we can do this together, we can take this bull by the horns. We can stop being victims of this curse. Everyone else is doing exactly that, waiting for the End. Let's fight back. Let's-' Lázaro sat next to the traveller and stared at him, imploringly. 'Let's do something about it, together.'

Something in Lorenzo's chest broke, and he knew that if the curse tried, his heart would be too weak to fight back.

'I don't have much time, kid, so let me tell you my story, even at risk of breaking your heart and leaving it as damaged as mine is right now.' The boy didn't understand. 'I come from Alpandeire, where I led a similar life as you did in Ronda during the cursed time. I took care of my grandmother, who was permanently stroking all of her dogs. No one could have ever taken her from those dogs! Little devils they were. Oh, and I also took care of my mother's grave. Everyday I would add a flower to her final resting place. There was a field of wildflowers by the time I... left.' Lázaro listened attentively, after all, he loved a good story. 'Everyone else seemed to be happy in their own way. I felt lonely, but was happy to be where I was. The sun didn't shine for us, we were safe in the protective shade of the mountains, away from this horrible orange doom.' Lorenzo continued, as the sunlight graced his cheeks, making his unexpected tears glisten. 'One day I climbed the church's bell tower. I used to like looking at all the little villages spreading through the land and imagining what people must have been doing there. I had no interest in finding out though, unlike you. As I said, I was happy to just be.' Lázaro thought that the traveller in the story didn't match the Lorenzo he knew. 'That was, until I saw the End-'

The boy reacted quickly to that affirmation. 'You couldn't have seen it from Alpandeire, the End is coming from the other side of the Sierra.' Lázaro was very confused.

Lorenzo gasped, took a second, then continued.

'At first I thought it must have been a cloud, some sand storm coming from lands far away. So I went to explore as it was approaching the neighbouring town of Jubrique... What I saw there was blood curdling. First a rain of ashes filled the land, the End draining all life from the nature around it. Then people started waking up from the curse when it was simply too late... They were devoured by the insatiable monster of darkness while crying, begging to all the saints in heaven, screaming, hopeless.'

He's been that close to it. He's seen it! Thought the boy, in awe and admiration.

'I ran for my life back to Alpandeire; I didn't stop once. I wanted to save my grandmother-' Lorenzo fought the tears back once more. He took a wavering breath. 'I couldn't carry her, she didn't want to leave all her dogs- I tried, Lázaro! I tried to bring her with me! As the ashes started to rain over Alpandeire I knew I had to leave. And I left, Lázaro. I just left her. I ran away from the End, in the opposite direction, as far as I could. At first I thought the End wouldn't be able to swallow whole mountains, so I thought myself safe.'

'But you came to Ronda? You came straight toward it?' Lázaro asked, bewildered.

Lorenzo nodded gravely.

'I ran away. It wasn't until you opened the Mondragón's curtains that I understood I was going straight into what I was running from.' The traveller moved his hand towards the sandy ground, with a fast movement, he drew a circle. Lázaro's jaw dropped as the traveller continued. 'The End is a circle. A damned circle that is getting smaller, eating everything it encounters. There's no escaping Lázaro, my cowardice has no reward. I betrayed my grandmother for nothing, and now I am betraying you, for you thought me something that I am not.' Lorenzo cried openly. 'I simply won't go to the End. I wish... I wish I was cursed! Like everyone else is!' He felt something releasing. He had given up control over his own body to an external force once again.

Lázaro's face became void of expression. Removing his calming hand from the traveller's back, leaving his side, the boy turned around and walked slowly. *He is speaking the truth, we are surrounded by the End*. The more Lázaro thought about it the more sense it made to him. *Of course it's a circle, of course we are trapped*.

Lorenzo continued to speak between sobs, not daring to look at his fellow adventurer, 'Speak to me, Lázaro! I'm telling you there's no need to get closer to the End! I've been there, there's only pain at the edge of the world!' Lorenzo covered his face, his chest hurting painfully, air struggling to reach his lungs. 'Please Lázaro! Let's hide somewhere safe.' The traveller's tears turned as red as the poppy flowers he used to take to his mother's grave. His sight, blurred by the crying blood, didn't impede him to see the tallest of doors right in front of him. He was seeing it with the eye of the mind. The door was carved out from a single chunk of wood, a masterful monolith. The orange sunlight seemed to reach that part of his illusion, as the mysterious entrance was covered by it. The traveller heard three loud knocks against the shining wood. Each one of them made him jump, scared. However he knew what he had to do, and so he placed his hands against the polished wood and pushed. Once the door opened just a bit, darkness embraced his insides. A loud bang of the door shutting tight returned him to the mill, to the river. The curse had finally locked itself inside his heart, and the world around him had lost all colour. From his black and white perception, he saw the boy leaving him behind. Possessed by pure evil, the stranger bolted and firmly grabbed Lázaro's arm. I *cannot allow him to leave, he needs to stay with me, forever. He cannot meet the End,* thought Lorenzo, cursed.

Lázaro tilted his face towards his, wordlessly, and pulled his arm from Lorenzo's grip. Then he turned and continued to walk away. 'Lázaro, please. I am sorry, boy. Don't leave me. You don't have to leave me. We'll stay here. Stay here with me, please. We'll wait, like everyone else. Please let's wait together. The End has freed us from time, this is our chance to live forever, boy. Time will only make your body grow old and weak.' Lázaro continued walking to the exit. 'You will see everything around you wither and die slowly. Stupid boy, stay I say!' Lorenzo begged in anguish, as he recognised some of his words weren't his. Some of the desperation he felt wasn't his.

Lázaro turned around one last time to look at the stranger's eyes, and there he found what he expected. The curse grew in his eyes, and the boy knew there was no salvation left for his friend. He felt heavy with disappointment, betrayed; not for the traveller's past actions, but for how Lorenzo had surrendered himself. The boy walked away, for the fire was burning brighter than ever and it had presented his heart with a new path. He had to face the End. He had to see it with his own eyes. He had to understand. Even if it meant doing so alone.

Before the boy left the ruined mill, he called back to the traveller, and spoke. 'Our nature does not change by will. I don't blame you. I forgive you. You did what you could. In fact, you brought change into my life. Possibility. That was all I needed to grow the courage to walk towards the sun.

Goodbye, Lorenzo.' And as the stranger fell to his knees, ready to wait, the boy departed, starting his pilgrimage towards oblivion.

Once he reached the outskirts of the forest, Lázaro heard a hopeless scream, closely followed by the rumbling of the ruined mill's roof collapsing.

He did not look back.
He looked up, as the ashes began to rain.

INTERLUDE - THE SHADOW

In which a cat explores an old palace; a Queen ends her toxic relationship;
and a ghost finds company.

A black shadow walked on top of the wall, carefully avoiding the vines that had grown over the centuries. Ronda's oldest site, the origin of the village, remained in the shade. Away from the cliffs, safe from the approaching sunset.

The black shadow jumped gracefully into a forgotten garden. This side of the village had been the beginning. The Celts, the first inhabitants and founders of Ronda, had followed a bright shooting star through many nights. They left the far North and ended up encountering the cliffs of their new home. They built the mines and a village, from which foundations rose to the place where the shadow roamed. Even older than the Mondragón Palace, a royalty worthy building stood wearily before the black shadow. Once splendorous, a paradise; now a derelict chaos of stone and wood that the villagers considered haunted by an old Moorish king, who did not treat their people with kindness. The destroyed palace oversaw a man-made canyon, the entrance to the deep mines that contained the river in its journey through Ronda.

The black shadow had no name, he was simply a shadow. A young cat that had never known a family, a home or any other form of love.

Don't be sad, reader, for you cannot miss what you do not know exists. The blackness of his fur was as dark as the End. His curiosity was as boundless as the land of the property he intended to visit before night arrived; not once questioning why he walked or his desire to explore the world around him. He followed his instincts and now, the old palace, once a King's dominion, was his playground.

The gardens were a miniature rainforest, as Shadow stalked through the grounds, he felt a collective gaze from many eyes. Tuning his senses, the cat clocked a flock of exotic bright yellow parrots that perched on top of the low trees. The birds observed him as he stealthily walked deeper into the dense maze. Shadow kept an eye on them, but he knew that they were harmless. Their multi-coloured feathers were now puffed up in preparation for the night. Their angry looking faces followed the cat as he passed by them.

Shadow knew he was the king of the realm, every building vulnerable to his advances, every human too unaware to notice a simple shadow. So he carried on walking, unknowingly, towards danger.

The branches above Shadow seemed to sway in warning. 'Hey shadow, stay in the realm of the light. Hey little shadow, stay in the realm of the living. Hey little shadow, don't bring back what's been forgotten.' Shadow did not speak their language.

A pool of water welcomed him into the heart of the paradise. Its unkempt surface, covered with life, impeded Shadow from uncovering the secrets below the stinking layer. The colourful tiles adorning the pond lost all their brightness under the shade of dusk. Turning around, he saw the silhouette of a well against the sky. The view from the forgotten gardens was stunning, as they hung over the cliffs. A vertical heaven for a feral kitten like himself.

A big statue of a peacock invited Shadow to investigate. The colours of the inanimate animal were the brightest the cat had ever seen. He admired the powerful beak, the little crown and the never ending tail. Following the piled

feathers, the multiple eye looking motifs made him wary of the statue. The cat, tricked by his curiosity, carefully approached his paw to grace the watching feathers. At the first playful touch of the cat's paw, the statue turned around to face him. The huge tail now raising, and then opening, to Shadow's astonishment. The cat jumped back, hissing, trying to puff his tail to compete with the living peacock. After staring at each other for a long moment, and dazzled by the beautiful tapestry of the feathered fan, Shadow decided that the wisest thing was to run away. Luckily the peacock did not follow, falling again into a deep statuesque sleep.

Rushing to find some shelter, Shadow found himself before a majestic door, made out of bronze and iron bars that slithered, interlinked and overlapped each other into the entrance. Time hadn't been easy on the building that now hung together by the grace of some forgotten god. The door was not attached to its frame anymore, but it was so heavy that it rendered the only way into the building blocked to robbers and curious children. Or at least until our dark friend found it. Looking back one last time, to ensure that the peacock wasn't following, the cat found a crack, a missing piece of the metallic puzzle at the bottom of the door. Shadow entered the former palace hoping for safety and more adventures.

As he disappeared from the garden, the plants, trees and branches whispered one last time. 'Hey little shadow, please let us sleep. Hey, you, uninvited shadow, don't make this darkness deeper.'

Shadow did not speak their language.

The building was rotting from the inside. The majestuous palace, former host of the greatest of candlelit dinners, matchmaker of the most romantic love stories, keeper of untold secrets, and witness of the cruellest betrayals - stood now in permanent decay, a shadow from what once was. A mirage in the middle of an oasis.

The entrance was a maze of fallen architecture, beams, splinters and spiders merged together in a room that used to welcome guests from everywhere around the world. Dodging the hanging beams, dust and sticky webs, the cat entered complete darkness. He followed the only thing that his senses could detect; a trickle of running water coming from inside the structure, an underground river was part of its very foundations. The cold gusts of air against his whiskers alerted him from the holes dotting the putrefied wooden floor. A free ticket to the river down below. A million spider eyes followed him as he traversed the dark.

After crawling under a chandelier that hung dangerously low, a door jamb leading to some light appeared in front of him. Shadow stopped to fastidiously lick the dust off his black fur.

Once clean, a new room dimly lit received him. The roof was missing, and the sun found its way in, enough light for Shadow to admire the grandeur around him. A portrait as big as a door oversaw the room, it boasted nothing but a blurred face, A man with stern eyes that seemed to follow the cat around the room. The carpet felt nice and soft under his paws, while tapestries covered the walls, showing different angles of Ronda's cliffs. Hexagonal tea tables remained carefully positioned around the chamber, hinting at what the kings and queens from the past did in there. As Shadow observed the painted visage, a voice talked to him.

'Hey little shadow, this palace was not built for you. Leave at once. I command you.' The voice seemed inviting, but Shadow did not comprehend those words. Not to mention that a cat will do whatever they want, not what they are told to do. The voice was ignored, and Shadow continued the exploration of the palace.

A side room opened to a twisted spiral staircase, a towering room with stone exposed in its walls, naked from ornaments. Clearly older than the rest of the palace, the smell of rot infested the place. The dampness in the air helped tiny moss grow in the cracks of every rock, every slope more slippery than the one before. At the centre of the spiral, a beheaded statue stood proud, its giant stone hand gripping a heavy spear. The grey colours of every part of the room, and the dim light coming from somewhere above, camouflaged the details of the statue. Shadow followed the weapon with his eyes, then he saw it; a terrible skull pierced by the aggressive metal point. The cat's fur stood up all over his spine, as his senses detected approaching trouble. Moving carefully, as to not disturb the centinel golem, the cat crossed the base of the tower in the staircase's direction.

'You should listen to my instructions, little fiend' The voice boomed across the tiny space of the stone room. 'Or I will have to bend you under my command.' Everything in the tower shook.

Shadow still did not know what it was saying, but this time he knew the voice meant danger. The statue's hand released the spear. Shadow saw it coming, but it was too late to jump back. The pierced skull fell, ready to hit the cat right in the head. A desperate hiss, a pointy tail and the attack was over. The killer spear and the skull missed the cat for a whisker, hitting the floor and making the whole tower shake. For a second, Shadow thought that the tower was unraveling over him. But silence came back, alas only briefly. Shadow couldn't recover from the scare, his fur still alert and his muscles locked. His instincts, however, had his cat brain calculating the best escape route from that infernal place. As he tried to gather momentum to jump towards the stairs, the slabs and tiles supporting the feline started to crack. The impact from the beheaded statue was too much for the structure to hold itself together, the tower trembled, and so did Shadow. The base of the room gave in, disappearing faster than the animal could have ever moved. A free fall welcomed him from underneath his paws. The cat should have indeed listened to the voice's helpful advice.

Shadow fell.

And as Shadow hurtled down the old tower, darkness embraced him. The stone falling with him hit the walls of the tower, creating sparks and smashing wall parts, which joined the descent and made it increasingly dangerous. The cat failed to hook his claws against any soft surfaces protruding from the darkness. Rubble and rocks hitting him everywhere.

The tiny moss and plants growing in the dark tried to provide some advice for the animal. 'Close your eyes, little shadow. The mines are sealed with its secrets, go to sleep with them, do not wake them up.' He was descending too fast to understand anything.

A deep vibration raised from the depths of the tower, a chant. The sound flooded the vertical tunnel, and by magic, illuminated the forgotten torches that covered the walls.

Blue fire crowning them. The cat started to float, as the descent decreased its speed. Rests of destroyed pulley works and rope remained as proof of the miners past existence. A gentle landing awaited him at the base of the tower. A cave-like room, sculpted into the bedrock of Ronda, with the remains of a water wheel as big as a house right at the centre of it; its lower half dissapearing into the bedrock, reaching for the icy water of the underground river. The blue fire from the torches up the tower illuminated the room, making Shadow feel like he was inside a precious sapphire. The vaulted ceiling reminded him of the sky. His paws against the cold and wet floor brought him back into his tiny body, almost forgetting about the thrill of the fall.

As he regained control of his tiny paws, he started to patrol the room, relieved that no possessed statues guarded the chamber. As he approached the round wall, out of thin air, a playful flame welcomed Shadow. At first dubious, then curious, the cat followed the floating blue fire, hopping around, trying to catch it, until they reached the far side of the circle room. The flame entered the wall, shining its bright blue light through the stone that held it. Only then he noticed a mosaic covering that side of the room, its tiles dimmed by the passing years. It would have remained invisible, if it wasn't for the eerie light coming from inside the palace, from the friendly wisp. The cat inspected the familiar landscape decorating the image. Ronda's cliffs in ancient times adorned this side of the wall, naked from any village, no bridge, no bullring. A pure virgin land, bracing for a menacing flaming rock parting the skies. When Shadow's eyes rested over the object in the sky, the light emanating from the palace grew brighter, making the cat hiss at the potential threat. The tiles started moving in front of the cat's eyes. A trail of the darkest smoke following the sky-stone, indicated an imminent impact against the primordial cliffs. A meteorite.

The blue within the wall disappeared before he could witness the impact, the tiles returning to its dimmed and aged appearance. In the darkness, the blue light reached Shadow from behind him, from the opposite side of the room. Shadow was trying to understand if the shiny things that moved inside the wall were real or not; his instincts kicked in, trying to figure out if the magic before his eyes was edible. The cat followed the cold light to the other side, where a second mosaic awaited; a throne room with a queen wearing a simple green dress, her face covered in boredom. Sitting next to her, a king so despicable that they had used red tiles to depict his eyes. The tense scene was completed by a group of miners, surrounding an object that Shadow could not comprehend. The miners' faces were filled with expressions of horror, covering their own eyes while opening their mouths in prayer. As the cat observed this scene, the lit wall raged in blue, and the miners moved to reveal the source of their despair: a stone as dark as ebony, the rock that fell from the skies, devoid from its destructive fire. Shadow followed the moving tiles with the utmost attention, not because he was invested in the story, but because that's what cats do. Right when the feline was about to jump against its prey, darkness enveloped him once again.

A third wall lit up, drawing the little shadow's attention. This time the decorated wall welcoming the cat showed the menacing ruler, wielding a powerful hammer, as he threatened with cracking the meteorite open. His face was full of pride and entitlement. The queen, still showing no emotion, observed from her throne, while the miners begged the king not to proceed with his intentions. As the blue fire within the walls raged once again, the hammer struck in a spectacle of sparks and smoke. Shadow sought refuge behind one of the stones connected to the central water wheel, as the deafening ringing of the hammer against the rock vibrated through the whole room. After the violent attack finished, the inside of the stone was revealed. Shadow left his hideout to see the contents of the rock, as they were shiny as anything he had seen before. At first, everyone thought that the brightness came from a crystal lodged within the burnt rock. Little they knew that the blinding light came from something sealed within the crystal itself. It was filled with a substance as dark as ink, where infinite galaxies and stars floated peacefully. The stubborn king had pierced the rock too deep - the crystal had been touched by its vengeful hammer, and now a tiny crack showed on its surface. The darkest liquid, seeking to be freed, spilled like blood from the sky-stone, slowly gracing the king's feet. The miners, having heard too many stories of evil falling from the sky, bowed to it, begging to be spared of the imminent danger they sensed.

And one last time, darkness and blue light swapped across the gigantic stone room. Shadow had learnt his lesson, and this time was the time when these moving tiles would end up clawed by his mighty paws. As soon as the blue light started to shine, Shadow ran in a hunting dash, determined to feed off the tasty looking tiles. The cat jumped with all his might against the wall. His paws catching the empty air, and the blue flame lighting up the palace's innards flickered, amused. A loud bang shook the central water mill, and the dome dropped tiny specs of dust and rock over the dizzy cat. The carefully laid tiles on the last wall bursted out everywhere - the sound of them bouncing over the floor filled the room. Shadow was too disorientated to understand what had happened. The feline took a second to recover from the blow, and shook his head as the remaining tiles started to glow blue by the flame's will. The bottom half of the picture was missing, but Shadow could see the king, completely covered by the black ink, lifting his fist clenching the crystal.

The queen was leaving the room, escaping in frustration and fear. Once the blue fire raged, the queen abandoned the mosaic. Shadow tried to follow her, but once the tiles stopped, the images vanished.

The central wheel in the room started turning, disappearing beneath the bedrock with a screeching sound that made Shadow flinch. The chant that accompanied him in his descent returned, even louder than before. The ghosts of the christian miners who succumbed to the king's greed rose. Everything went bright blue.

'You should have let us rest, little fiend. You will now come to sleep with us. We put our story on the walls to avoid this!' the voices elevated across the blue room, as the ceiling started to crack and unravel, threatening to seal the mine's entrance forever.

Shadow expertly dodged the rain of boulders that destroyed anything they touched. The wheel turned one last time, as the mosaic's disembedded themselves from the walls. The room cracked everywhere. A nutshell opening in violence. The room collapsed, but the cat never gave up and so he raced towards a fresh crack on the walls. Shadow followed his instincts, adventuring deep into the hole in the wall, while everything he left behind became rubble. It wasn't long before the loud destruction became absolute silence.

His tiny body could feel the exhaustion from all the falling, running, escaping and exploring he had been doing. His hurting paws found a cold relief when the ground started to become wet. A rushing sound followed, revealing to him that he had reached the river flowing underneath the cliffs of Ronda. The cat, not having anywhere else to go, continued to follow the tight crack, in the direction in which the water was flowing.

The familiar noise of a rushing stream echoed through the caverns as Shadow followed the tunnel, until he found its source. From the top of the ledge where Shadow stood, a few metres over the room's floor, he could see a powerful stream cascading over a massive stone slab decorated with carvings of flowers. The slab appeared to be as new as when it was first sculpted, filled with writing in a language that was not spoken in Ronda any more. At the feet of the stone, on the bed of a shallow lake, sat a simple vault made out of the same stone. The last resting place of the tyrant, within the depths of the Earth and almost a thousand feet underneath Ronda's very Bullring. Not detecting any danger, Shadow jumped into the room.

The final cave was worthy of a king; illuminated thanks to a naturally formed chimney, so high, that the sun above could filter and reflect through the cracks and polished surfaces. The ceiling was high and the stone created beautiful arches, turning the room into a natural cathedral. Flowing water, surging from every wall, had carved and eroded the shapes into the rock over a thousand years. The stone was surrounded by celtic symbols repeated over and over, painted white into the walls and visibly more ancient than anything else in the room. Circles and triquetras looping the majestic structure into a sacred place, evidence that humans had reached that spot underneath the village years ago, understanding its future importance. The king had invaded the holy chamber by burying himself and his unholy sky-stone on it. His workers tried to hide the unholy place by sharing its story in the mosaics that preceded the tomb. They did not account for a shadow to reach their deepest secret.

As Shadow's curiosity spiked again, the cat approached the vault. Before he could take a step into the shallow lake, a new voice returned, only that this time it was very close. 'Little shadow, you don't know what you are about to unleash. Let the evil rest. Come with me.'

As the cat turned around, he discovered the Queen, in her beautiful green dress and with a powerful and desperate stare. 'I command you,' she said softly. But Shadow thought it would be a good idea to clean himself right at that precise moment. He hadn't been following the royal drama, and his fur was a complete mess. The Queen was gone.

After he did his best to tidy up by using his tongue and water from the shallow lake, something twinkled in the feline's peripheral vision. He was immediately enraptured, this time nothing would escape to his trained claw.

On top of the stone vault, a tiny light shone. Shadow's instincts were completely alert, excited to finally catch a prey that day. He leapt around the monument trying to entrap the glowing dot, as if playing with a stray ray of sun. Appearing and disappearing, the little point of light playfully deceived the animal. As the cat crouched, he noticed a black liquid spilling from inside the vault. Shadow didn't pay attention to it, he was about to score a catch. And so he plunged against the titling reflection. At the touch of his paw against the tiny constellation, Shadow disappeared from the world in an instant. For the light was the singularity. The origin. The centre of the diminishing horizon.

The light was the curse.

A flight of swallows froze in the chilling air of sunset. Never escaping the approaching Winter. Never leaving; therefore never again returning to the golden cliffs of Ronda.

The curse had been unleashed.

The ghost of the terrible king welcomed the cat to the afterlife, and they made great company for one another as they watched the End unfold.

VIII - THE PALM READER

In which Lázaro is committed but still scared of witches; a poet is awake; and the boy meets the swallows.

As Lázaro walked towards the sun, the frozen star seemed to extend from one extreme of the horizon to the other, more imposing than ever. The ash had stopped raining as he got closer to the source. Remnants of the grey dust still tangled in his hair and clothes. The orange light was so bright by now that he could barely keep his eyes open - not even by closing them the boy could escape the regent sun. White, orange and pink flares tormented his pupils through his eyelids. The stained landscape had become a surrealist wasteland; the mountains wholly absent, the dried earth cracked in endless veins below his feet, and not a single soul was to be seen. Monuments to the former glories of trees and plants waved to the whirls of sinister gusts. The wind seemed to carry a message of caution - a damp coldness against the scorching sunset. *That wind came straight from the End.* His pilgrimage to the boundary of existence was not over, not just yet. The fire still burning inside his heart felt like dancing in brotherhood with the ominous light. All around the boy, dust motes succumbed chaotically to the final wind, that in turn, traversed past the boy's ears, creating a constant lacerating sound. Lázaro could almost hear the screams of the dead buried beneath his feet.

'*Keep walking, keep walking, boy,*' his ancestors, united with the soil, cheered Lázaro from within the white noise of the curse. '*She's close. Keep walking,*' the boy seemed to hear words braided in the wind. A product from his fertile imagination, he assumed. Defying the dark horizon rising ahead, and comforted by the voices in the wind, the boy kept moving forward. The young one's heart raced every single time he pictured the last step into the nothing.

The land beneath his feet rumbled occasionally, which he took as another warning of the End's proximity. The final line of darkness, once raging at a distance, was now closer than ever, revealing its secrets without shame. The boy held his chin up high, heading straight against the ethereal and slithery wall. From his vantage point he observed the horizon's behaviour. Its texture and its shape seemed to change every second; from an emerging tidal wave ready to flatten the land, to an almost see-through cloud. It resembled, at times, the kind of mist that came in sliding down the mountains of Ronda after night fell. Even at times resembling a giant dying snake, squirming and raising parts of its body in pain. It felt like seeing a ghost, like having a dream. The End wasn't supposed to be there, still, there it was, about to devour the whole village.

Will I be able to walk past it? Or will it be as solid as the cliffs in Ronda? Hopefully it will be soft as a whisper, Lázaro wondered, as he witnessed the impossible line spread before his eyes.

The malevolent dark snake divided itself at times, crowns jumped towards the clouds, arching like dragon wings soaring the skies; the kid had nothing against such a power. He noticed the ground had started to shake following a pattern, a rhythm. Lázaro imagined a whole army of death cloaked inside the End, conquering reality one step at a time. The rhythm seemed to counter the cheering from his ancestors laying below him. Suddenly, a feeling.

What is this coldness, this emptiness I feel? Wondered the boy as his inner bonfire receded to embers. The brooch of light had become invisible.

The dark horizon was ready to claim its prey.

This feeling does not belong to me... where does it come from?
Lázaro asked, as he understood. An insatiable hunger. An invincible enemy who craved life. It craved for every thing that had ever been touched by time, for time was once part of its dominion, part of pure nothingness. Lázaro's stomach crawled as feelings began to emerge inside his body.

This is not me. I am not this. You are not bringing me down with you- an emotional invasion by an unknown force, upwards from his guts. Those feelings weren't his own. They talked to him about revenge, filled him with despair and pierced his chest with hunger. Tears bloomed in his eyes, as the End's feelings made themselves comfortable in their new flesh. Lázaro kept pushing through the land, power-walking against the End's attempts to seize its victims.

'I shall palliate the hunger that devours us all with my own body, with my own soul.' Lázaro walked faster, shielding his eyes from the piercing sun beams. Not much was left around him, other than the scattered remains of what once was a lush valley filled with nature. An abandoned clothing line with its white linen, socks and pants was being pulled violently by the wind, fluttering helplessly in every direction, standing precariously as a reminder of the people who had already succumbed to hunger. Then, a voice clearer than the ones carried in the wind reached the boy. The boy halted.

That voice, I did not imagine it.

Wrenched from his dark thoughts, the boy grew aware of his surroundings, trying to identify where the words came from. Secretly hoping that it didn't mean a threat to his pilgrimage.

'Hey kid, where do you think you're going!?' Although it was no louder than a whisper, the voice projected past wind and noise with undeniable authority and sharpness. Lázaro reluctantly moved his gaze from the sun to the source of the question. He squinted at the nearby silhouette, waiting for his eyes to adjust; a sunken tree, so dry that it was ivory white. A person resting against it. A small figure completely covered by multiple colourful fabrics dancing in the wind. The boy wondered if he had stepped into a mirage at the end of the world.

'Yes, you. Why are you running? It looks like you're running away from a ghost. Where are you going, eh?' The robed person spoke, denoting a voice that belonged to an old lady. Lázaro stood still, about to skip this distraction and resume his journey.

'That way there's only death... why would such a youthful spirit be wanting to finish it all sooner than his time?' the woman pondered out loud, catching Lázaro's attention. She fixed him a look and Lázaro felt scrutinised from his intentions to the deepest corners of his soul. The old lady's many different layers of colourful garments were thrown over one another, in no apparent order. A veil covered her head, with a few strands of black hair framing a weathered face. Her eyes were striking, easily the most beautiful shade of grey he had ever seen, glistening under the dimming light of the sun.

'Oh! You lost the power for words didn't you! Ha!' The lady laughed, beckoning the boy over with a couple quick hand movements. 'Come here, my boy!' The woman shifted weight from one leg to the other, as if her old bones could not keep her standing upright for much longer.

Lázaro wasn't sold, after all, everyone who inhabited that part of the region ought to be long gone. *She just laughed like a witch. Maybe she's another witch. I may be in trouble.* The boy thought as his body followed the directions of the shady lady, rather than his own commands. *This witch is different from the one by the bonfire. Why am I not terrified?* Lázaro asked himself as he remembered his mother's cautionary tales. A sudden sadness almost completed the emptiness within him. She had always told him about the hunting sessions witches held to capture children, sacrificed them to nameless demons living in their hearts and then ate them while the kids' blood was still warm. Back then, Lázaro had spent more than one night crying, now fear had calcined his heart. Only embers and hunger remained. Aware of this, the boy regained control of his actions, breaking from the old lady's magical grip.

'Hello ma'am, I am walking towards the sun. Even if no one wants to take action, I will.' Lázaro stated clearly as he advanced with resolution in his eyes, defying the strange presence. Raising her gaze, the old lady looked into the

175

boy's eyes.

'Wise words for such a young soul.'

'What even does young and old mean these days, in a land of no time?' Lázaro replied curtly. 'My thoughts have been trapped for so long inside this body, they are now those of someone hundreds of years old.' His words tinged with threat, his light piercing through from within.

'Look at you! You really do seem to know a lot more than this old woman,' she exclaimed as she took her hands to her forehead in surprise. An array of bracelets and trinkets clashed as they dropped down her bony arms. 'You must be exhausted carrying all that knowledge, come here, help me take a seat on this dead tree trunk. Let me provide a bit of respite before you meet your end, brave boy.' The old lady wasn't fazed by the boy's confident tone. Summoning Lázaro's politeness was more powerful than any magic, so the boy obeyed.

The young one noticed her robes swung as if disconnected from her movements, like she was drifting in water. With a couple grunts, the lady found herself comfortable atop the white tree. She looked at Lázaro mysteriously, then pinched the boy's chin, angling his head against the light so as to appreciate his features in detail.

'What a shame, so young, so full of life!' Lázaro wasn't happy to be treated like a toddler, but just as he was about to defy the old lady, she changed her demeanour. She started to answer the boy's many questions, even before he could have asked them. 'I am a seer, a palm reader. I've travelled the world looking for a soul who knows what this curse is, why it is happening, and how to defeat it. Sadly not many were even aware of its existence, you know? Anyway those people who were aware, like you and myself, led me to Ronda.' A shadow of realisation covered the palm reader's eyes. 'My hip was about to give up, I had no way to make it to the village and find out the truth for myself. Now I realise why. We were meant to meet at this place,' sentenced the truth sayer as the puzzled boy opened his mouth.

'Stop talking in riddles, please. Who else is awake? How can Ronda hold the truth? I just came from there, and nothing looks one bit like the truth!' Lázaro demanded impatiently. The lady laughed again. 'Ha! How cute! First things first, love, we still have a bit of time around this tree trunk. Like I said, a bit of respite.'

Lázaro then noticed that time was flowing differently around the woman. *She has brought time back!*

'I met a couple of 'awake' people, like you call them, ha! How cute. Three including yourself, actually. The three of you have been awakened indeed.' She had hooked the boy with her bait, but she was not reeling.

I need to know more! Lázaro thought as the hunger growing inside him demanded more knowledge. 'Who were the other two? What do you know about the End that could aid me in my journey?' Lázaro asked urgently, politeness and patience abandoning his body.

'The End... Is that what you call it? Honestly, too cute! Such an inappropriate name!' Not deciphering any mysteries, brushing past the big answers Lázaro expected, she continued. 'Let's make a deal, yes? You let me do what I do best and in exchange I shall tell you the stories of the people I got to meet, yes?' The lady hid her hands away inside the many folds of her clothes and produced a red handkerchief. The boy was brimming with even more questions.

'What do I have to do? What do you do best?' He spurted without much thought, incapable of choosing between all of his ideas.

'Yes, yes of course, what I do best is palm reading. I told you didn't I? So what, deal or not my dear? We have a bit more time but not a lot, as you can probably guess from looking at... the End.' Lázaro had nothing to lose, and he had to know as much as he could before his final encounter with the endless darkness. The boy extended his right hand in offering to the seer.

'Left one always, love, cannot learn much from the right things. Rather learn from the wrongs, Ha!' the witch's laughter almost resurrected fear from its ashes. He switched hands, willing to pay a high price for knowledge. 'Don't be afraid, love. It's too late for mischief now. I mean no harm.' The lady grabbed Lázaro's hand. The touch felt electric. Her skin felt unexpectedly soft, like silk, decorated with inky motifs that reminded Lázaro of the wooden ceiling of the Mondragón palace. The breeze picked up, and the eerie wind blew about their clothes and hair. The kid lowered himself to his knees, attempting to shield from the rising dust. The seer stared deeply into his eyes, her fingers tracing invisible glyphs on the top of his palm. She had created a bubble of time, and the boy was breathing like a baby who was using his lungs for the first time. A lightning without thunder struck the pair. Absolute silence, only her words.

'Now listen to the story as I look into your soul, my dear.'

Their eyes met, there wasn't any escape, he was hers.

This knowledge better satisfy my borrowed hunger, Lázaro thought, as the palm reader seemed to trace every single crease time had created in his skin.

'I met people who were not linked by the curse twice before yourself. One of them, a powerful woman, a mourning widow, dressed all in black. She lived in a little town near my cave, by Granada. After realising that the thing you call the End was coming, she locked her five youthful darling daughters inside her big farmhouse. Trying to protect them, such a mother! The curse hit her, and she would not open the doors for her daughters, forever protecting them. The sad thing is that her daughters weren't affected by this damned curse. They grew bored within those walls, not knowing the source of their mother's fears. Not knowing that the End was coming. Unaware of how their mother was shielding them,' the palm reader pushed one of her long nails against Lázaro's skin, until she drew blood. Lázaro hissed. 'The pretty girls couldn't do anything to escape what to them was tyranny. They decided to end things their own way. Escaping. Jumping. You know what I mean... you've tried it yourself.' An image of death and despair flashed in front of Lázaro. 'Instead of escaping, they got themselves trapped for good. You see, love, the only way to break the curse is to remove what anchors you to this world. The mother woke up once she had nothing to protect. I read her palm just like I'm reading yours right now. Out of compassion. Poor woman. She must have joined her girls by now. Forever trapped, until the very end.'

As the lady passed her slender fingers across each and every crease in Lázaro's hand, vivid images of the daughters flooded his mind. Their whole lives invaded Lázaro as much as the End did before. When they felt love, when they felt sisterhood. A window. A high beam. A scream. He shivered while remembering that he had been quite close to ending things by his own hand. An explosion of feelings raptured in the small vessel of his body. Tears appeared in his eyes, once again produced by emotions that were not his.

'As I was leaving the condemned farmhouse, I heard someone crying,' the palm reader proceeded. 'But there wasn't much around. No there wasn't. Then I saw a dried up well in the middle of the moor. And I found inside the most unusual thing, a young man crying his eyes out, the poor soul!' The palm reader turned Lázaro's hand, and started to look at his nails in fastidious detail. 'Yes, yes, he was the second person not affected by the curse.' The lady smiled.

'So close to one another?' Lázaro questioned, perplexed. 'Why do you think that was?'

The Earth rumbled again, and the palm reader stopped her ritual for a second. Reaching the ground with her free hand, she felt the vibrations of the earth. Closing her eyes, she muttered, 'It's moving again'. Then she continued talking, at a faster pace.

'Not sure at all, love, but I suspect the love of a mother is strong enough to shield a whole village from this curse... Anyhoo, my dear, let me tell you what he told me. This young man was actually not of sound mind, he was a poet you see, and he said he was in love with everything and he couldn't bear it all, it was too much.' The seer grabbed a piece of red fabric and ripped off her garments. Then proceeded to bandage the boy's hand.

'He was crying about the girls in the house, he loved them all too much you see. But then, he told *it* to me. Something I knew already, but him being a poet helped me understand better. He used words to explain it beautifully. A metaphor of magic. I understood it all.' A silent lightning struck again. There was nothing in the world but both of them.

'So, listen carefully, my dear,' the seer said as she yanked the boy's arm, getting his head close to him, ready to pour an unholy truth directly into his ear. She covered her mouth, as if telling him a secret, and whispered. 'We are swallows flying across the darkest night:

One day we find an open window, and the warmth of a house beckons us, so we enter. Inside, everything is lit up by a hundred golden candles, with their light illuminating the most wonderful treasures you can imagine. Golden frames of fantasy landscapes, goblets and whatnot. In that house, some may receive good food and meet other sparrows, some may get nothing from the experience, and some may simply observe the astonishing paintings hanging on the wall... The thing is, we have to leave at some point, and there are rules on how to do that. We need to fly out through the same window we came in. We need to meet the same darkness once again.'

At this point, the lady stopped whispering to his ear and stared back to his face, into his soul. Do you understand poetry, Lázaro? Can you see the sacred truth that lies beneath the metaphor? If you can't, you will, for I've found what I needed to know. Ronda held the truth after all, Ronda held you.' Lázaro's spine shivered. He realised he hadn't told the woman his name.

'Witch,' he whispered back at her. The land rumbled, stronger this time.

'And now listen even more carefully, Lázaro!' Said the woman, clasping both his hands tightly. 'Some of the swallows happen to fall asleep within the room, drink something poisonous and die, or perhaps the owner of the house may stroll around and step on them unintentionally. If any of that takes place, if they don't leave the room by the means they came in... In that case the sparrow will always remain under the painful light. Dead or not. Eternally. Restless. Only light.'

She closed her eyes and stood up. The dying sun shone right behind her. Lázaro could not distinguish her features against the cursed sunshine. He tried to process the poet's tale, but he wasn't sure he fully understood anything yet.

The lady opened her eyes again, greener and brighter than before. She released the boy's hands and hid hers underneath her clothes. Her job was done, she was ready to share with him what she discovered in the creases of his palm.

'All the lines in everyone's hands are fading. You may not see it, but it's clear for any palm reader. Yours, however, are the strongest I've seen since the curse arrived.' As her eyes went blank, words that were not her own sprang off her tongue. 'You will see through the veil and won't have enough coins to pay the fare. But worry not, for I know your many names. I will take care of that. You have transcended time and space many times before, and you will, once more. King of kings.' The lady abruptly kissed the back of his left hand, lowering her frame as if to kneel before royalty. Lázaro's heart was racing, the hunger growing deeper and thicker by the second. Then it happened, the ground rumbled as the End accelerated its raging march. With the power of millions of soldiers, wanting to conquer the last human bastion, the soil cracked and broke under the pair's feet. The lady grabbed Lázaro's hands once again, maintaining the connection to the clairvoyant's trance. The boy looked back to the far away cliffs, and what he saw scared him to his core; the rocks that made Ronda were slowly crumbling. The cliffs divided and threw themselves against the distant floor. Lázaro continued trying to release himself from the woman's grip, but the quake had passed before he managed to move even one of her bony fingers. Looking back once again, he saw that Ronda remained. He could not assess the destruction from where he was, but the bridge remained. *I have to meet the End before it's too late. I'll do it for them.*

The palm reader relaxed, as her eyes returned to a calming green, and the bubble of time bursted. The curse was back, once again. Lázaro's lungs failed to adapt to the air, as time around him dissipated once again.

'So, now everything is in your hands. What are you going to do, my dear? Are you going to *jump* outside from that window, or are you going to wait for the owner of the room to give you a good smack?' She threw her head back in a fit of hysterical laughter that chilled Lázaro to the bone. He turned around and started running towards the horizon, sorting the profound gaps the rumble had created in the dried up land. He couldn't understand anything.

'Your actions will be so bold, my dear! So bold that someone, somewhere, is writing about you this very second!' Shouted the seer, waving goodbye. 'Remember what happens to the sparrows who sleep!' She shouted, as she became smaller and smaller, until Lázaro couldn't see her anymore.

IX - THE BRIDGE

In which a house needs an exorcism; wax get spilled on the floor;
and a scream chases its owner.

Lorenzo, trapped within his own cursed heart, managed to use the last of his strengths to scream. The piercing wailing pushed time forward for a second. It bounced violently against the walls of the building, and a second was all the time the precarious structure needed to collapse. The withered stones balancing the wooden beams and the red tiles came down over the grieving man. The slabs and rocks hit him in the head and rendered him unconscious, helpless. Then, as he remained knocked out, time abandoned the derelict mound - even after the building was no more, the echo of the scream continued to vibrate in the air around the riverbend. It would never go out, it would always hang open and suspended as a witness of Lorenzo's cowardice. Like a ghost, prying over the traveller's body.

Lorenzo woke up, startled by his own scream. *Who is screaming? Who is in that much pain?* The traveller thought as he surveyed the nearby woods and the rubble all around him. A layer of red dust covered the traveller's face and hands, his clothes ragged by the collapse, his head hurting and wounded. The traveller looked above from where he was, astonished at the realisation that the origin of the scream was no other than himself. *I remember, the curse had me, and in the last moment I... I screamed at the top of my lungs.* Lorenzo observed the consistency of the air in front of him, carefully following the movement of the sound, as he regained full reign over his legs and arms. Over his heart.

When he stood up, brushing the specks of dust and stone off his body, a blunt pain appeared over his left eye. The pain came from within his skull, deep inside behind his left eyebrow. The traveller took a hand and placed it against his eye, rubbing it with a sigh. *This pain is killing me, the blow must have been bad. And this endless scream is not helping!* Assessing the potential damage his body had suffered, he realised something. His heart, as cracked, broken and fragile as it was, did not hold the curse anymore. *I can't believe it was as easy as that. An honest scream and that curse was gone... I need to tell Lázaro... Lázaro!? I can't believe I had forgotten about him! He must be about to meet the End. I need to-* His thoughts interrupted by a blunt hit in the back of his head. It missed its target, like a bird of prey whose talons failed to capture a scared mouse. It felt like a bird was attacking him. Ready to fight the unexpected attacker, he looked all around trying to identify the threat. Surveying the trees carefully, the scream grew strangely louder. Turning around his head, he found what he was looking for; the curse.

He could hear it approaching, menacing, invisible; waves of pure hate that spreaded through the air. A buzz, an electric current suspended and open. Alerted, he finally discovered the origin of his expelled nightmare; the visible vibrations surrounding the sound. As it floated through the air, it produced a wavy illusion similar to the heat that came from the pavement during a hot Summer day.

Lázaro would have loved to witness the curse under this disguise, thought the traveller, as the mention of the boy made his heart crack once again. His headache intensified. The cursed scream, patiently waiting for the right moment to attack once again, sensed that Lorenzo had let his guard down and charged against him, trying to reclaim his body. The traveller stepped back and tripped with the wooden beam that hit him in the head. He fell on his rear, as he dodged the attack from the high-pitched scream. The sound and its owner stared at each other, duelling, calculating their every move. *I need to run away, back to Ronda. If I leave this sound behind, perhaps I can find a safe place to shield myself from the End! Or maybe I should go stop Lázaro before-* Another crack, his heart was succumbing. The scream launched itself against the traveller's mouth, filling it with air and rage. Lorenzo started to wrestle against its own pain, as he started to feel the scream sliding down his throat. The closer the curse was to his heart, the more he only thought about Lázaro and the less he could do to resist the invasion. *I need to forget about that boy. I need to erase him from my memory. And fast!*

Struggling against the scream, Lorenzo used his whole will power to push Lázaro away from his mind. He visualised him walking towards the End, stepping over thin air and falling; disappearing forever. Lorenzo screamed once again, so hard that his mouth tasted like iron and blood. The sonic invasion repelled by the defenseless traveller. From that moment, Lázaro disappeared. Every memory inside his mind, locked away in a deep dark cell from which no thoughts could escape. Lorenzo grew colder and colder, getting rid of any emotion. The scream, however, started to grow louder again, ready for a new attack.

This time the traveller stood up and started running in the sun's opposite direction. He could still hear the terrible sound trapped in the air as he put some distance between himself and the ruined mill. *I wonder, if it will chase me if I run away.* Feared Lorenzo, numb, as the cliffs of Ronda appeared in front of him.

Feeling more of a stranger than the first time he arrived at the village, he started to climb the steps leading to the old village of Ronda. *I feel like I've forgotten something important, but I'm not sure what it is,* thought Lorenzo, not being aware that what he was lacking was his loyal fellow adventurer, Lázaro. The impossible fortress stood proud, the last bastion against an unavoidable ending. The bronze sheen of sunlight still covered the rock that sustained the town. Ronda was the final place on Earth to be forgotten forever. Lorenzo took in the sight of the powerful bridge and how it fused the two sides of Ronda together, admiring once again the craftsmanship of the monument. The many steps leading to the old town did not tire him like they did before- he felt nothing. He didn't care any longer.

A loud shout startled the traveller.

'You ended up getting lost right? I knew it! Young people these days have forgotten how to listen to their superiors.' The scaffolding started to shake as the man continued projecting his deep voice. 'I wonder if this beauty would be standing here today if I hadn't listened to my father!' Exclaimed a deep voice from above Lorenzo's head. The builder who welcomed him to Ronda stood in the exact same position, doing exactly the same action, than the first time they met. He was endlessly repairing his family's treasure, the great bridge.

'Forgive me good man! I actually ended up finding the Mondragón. Now I'm looking for some shelter. Do you know which is the safest place in Ronda, perhaps?' Asked

Lorenzo, trying to determine his final resting place.

'Are you saying that Ronda is a dangerous place? You better rethink that, we're all like family here,' challenged the builder.

'No, good sir. I've heard there's a bad Summer storm coming this way. What place in the village could withstand the force of wind, rain and thunder?' Lied Lorenzo, as he grew more desperate to find the perfect hiding place.

'A Summer storm, huh? Good, the fields need some water, it hasn't rained for too long around here. About your question; what do you expect me to say? Of course it is she! I've made this bridge who she is. There's not a more stable structure in the whole of the region. If there's a safe place, that is she!' Exclaimed the builder proudly, as he started to explain the intricacies of the bridge's internal works. Lorenzo didn't understand everything, but if he had to wait for the End, he would do it with a roof over his head.

'Nah sir, I don't plan on staying in the rain, no matter how safe the bridge will be,' replied Lorenzo, as he resumed his ascension to the old village.

'Wrong again, this youth. There's a big room built inside

our bridge you see. You follow those little steps down the other side of the cliff, and then the door should be open.' Explained the builder, pointing at the other side of the gorge. 'There's two beautiful french windows, one to each side of the bridge, that have the best view of the fields in town. It used to be a prison back then, you know? Still, the very best views of the land!' Shared the proud builder, happy at the chance of bragging about the work of a lifetime.

Lorenzo felt safe at the thought of going into prison. *Locked away from all the darkness around us*– 'And you would be kind enough to allow me to spend the night in that room, sir?'

'Are you calling us bad people again, stranger? Of course you can stay there. That room was more than a prison; at one point it was a hospital, it was a refuge for lost souls like you, and even an archive. I've either heard of or remember many, many other functions, some go way back to before my father was born. That room is not mine, it's Ronda's.' The builder found the traveller's surprised expression amusing. He looked down with a threat in his eyes, frowning his tanned face, showing wrinkles as deep as the canyon below them. 'Now, harm my bridge, and I promise you I'll drop your body down from the highest point of the cliff!' Lorenzo understood the threat as a tactless joke, and faked a laugh. The builder laughed as well.

'That's where I'll go then my kind sir. Thank you ever so much.'

'Don't mention it, youngster, just be sure to share how kind the people of Ronda were to you, wherever you may go.' Lorenzo nodded in agreement. 'I'll be working until the sun leaves the horizon, and be back up as soon as the sun rises. You know where to find me.'

'Yes sir, thanks so much again, sir,' repeated Lorenzo in reverence at the builder's kindness. *That's where I will wait for the End to declare its victory,* thought the stranger as he turned around, leaving the builder to his never ending building.

Meanwhile in Ronda, a girl opened her eyes for the first time since the curse commenced. She had been in the main church of the old village, an austere chunk made out of stone borrowed from the city's cliffs, with not much decoration other than an intricate steeple. She had fallen a victim to the curse while devotedly praying to an image of the Virgin Mary, hoping to heal the emotional pain of an unrequited love. As she continued with her looped prayer, an earthquake shook the whole building, provoking the hanging chandeliers to dance and cracks to emerge all over the ceiling. The young girl ignored it, lost in her request to the Virgin, until the shaking threw one of the praying candles all over the marble floors, spilling wax everywhere. The tinkling of the metal against the cold stone was what made her open her eyes, not very happy about the interruption. She quickly took the candle and placed it in its original position in front of the crying Virgin. She then closed her eyes and returned to her prayers, as if the world wasn't ending.

A hawk observing the town of Ronda from above wouldn't have noticed anything wrong; ladies saying goodbye to another day, hello to another night. The puchero stews boiling in preparation for dinner, filling the alleyways with the smell of celery. Beds being prepared for the night, labourers trying to find their way back home after a long day in the fields. Kids playing in the streets, clinging to the last rays of sun. People praying to gods that no longer existed. A gently whistled melody, coming from lips nowhere to be seen. The same actions over and over. The monumental bullring stood proud of the death it had held. A circle of oblivion, no less impressive than the End itself. Builders and miners, kings and corpses, animals and ghosts, lights and shadows, all of them awaited the End without knowing it. They would be asleep for it, though. As asleep as a little swallow in the brightest room, vulnerable, weak.

The End was too close now.

Three old ladies were sitting in their chairs watching the sun swell. They were silent as the earthquake began looking sideways at each other in unconfessed panic. It was a brief but contundent shake. Maria exploded in laughter as soon as the earthquake passed, not really knowing how to react to something that was not part of their condemned routine. Lorenzo entered the old village at that precise moment, regaining balance after the tremor. *Who could be laughing so obscenely at the end of the world? How could anyone be this self absorved? - Thinking it twice, at least it is not a scream,* the traveller realised, his spine chilling at the thought of the damned wailing he had left behind. He felt like screaming again, but he had no malediction left to expel from his body. His path towards the bridge took the stranger past the three old women. Hesitant at first, Lorenzo resolved to walk right past them.

'I can't believe your husband fell for such a silly move. Bless him in heaven!' Said Maria with watery eyes.

'Yes, woman!' carried on Perpetua. 'He was snoring so loud he shook the house more than that sad earthquake just did! I couldn't even sleep anymore, so I looked at him, aimed, and slapped him so hard that my hand hurt for days! Then I pretended to be as asleep as I could be. Honest to God!' The women couldn't stop laughing, as Lorenzo tried to tiptoe past them without grabbing their attention. 'Oh dear, my poor saint of a husband was terrified of ghosts ever after. He swore that he had seen a vengeful anima attacking him in the middle of the night, while I was peacefully asleep!' Perpetua could not finish her story, as her belly started to ache from laughing too hard.

'Oh lordy, lordy, lordy- I still remember the face of Father Jacobo when your poor husband asked him to exorcise the house!' Eustaquia added, as the three burst once more into refreshed laughter remembering the priest's reaction.

Lorenzo was about to leave them behind, unnoticed, when Perpetua saw him. She shushed her companions, and a steely silence fell across the pebbled street. The three ladies stared at him.

Perpetua cleared her throat and asked 'And who is this supposed to be?'

Lorenzo shivered before the question. I *am nothing more than a coward seeking refuge from my own cowardice,* an intrusive thought, a truthful answer. His mind went blank and he couldn't think of anything to say.

Maria, in aid of the traveller, lightly hit Perpetua in her wrist and scolded her for her manners.

'Pardon Perpetua, stranger, and welcome to Ronda. We just haven't seen any new faces in Ronda for quite some time now.' Maria added as the land shook slightly once again. The hungry rumble of the End's belly.

He was still lost for words, *these tremors are only getting worse, I need to reach the bridge promptly! I just know it's the place where I need to be. My final resting place.* Lost in his looming thoughts, Lorenzo looked quite silly standing there, saying nothing.

Eustaquia could smell a secret from miles away. She knew something was wrong with the traveller standing nervously in front of them. So readjusting her black shawl and frowning inquisitively, she leaned close to better the traveller to observe him.

'You seem like you know stuff, stranger. Stuff that we don't know. And I don't like not knowing things. What's your business in this town, huh?' The woman said while squinting her eyes at him, almost seeing through his flesh and into his broken heart.

She instilled such fear in the poor lost soul of Lorenzo! He was so scared that she would actually see him for what he was, that he started to spurt words at random, hoping to satiate the questioning lady.

'Yes, you're right my dear m'am. Yes. I am indeed here to visit the Mondragón. They are really good friends. I came to meet their daughter, Talita.' Lorenzo lied, not really knowing why he would mention his damned father.

'Ugh, the Mondragón!' Exclaimed Perpetua in disgust, puckering her lips at the thought of the landlord. 'They take everything and thank nothing! Years and years that they've done their will with this town, without caring for any living soul in the cliffs, the mines, the river or the fields. Curse them!' She said as she spat on the floor. Lorenzo knew he had made a mistake. The stranger was about to get a good rant from the angelic looking old ladies, when a loud scream arose from down the cliffs, stopping the interrogation on its tracks.

'Sor Angela...' Muttered María in prayer.

'What in the world was that?' Continued Eustaquia.

'I have no clue, was it a pig? It's around this time of the year that the farmers do their slaughtering,' wondered Perpetua, as the wailing continued; closer this time.

Lorenzo knew exactly whose scream that was. Taking advantage of the diversion, the traveller turned around and ran down the street. He didn't know how to get to the great bridge of Ronda, so he followed a sensation. A strange magnetism that pulled him toward his destination, navigating him through the maze of narrow streets. He moved as if he knew them by heart. Under the silent stare of the seemingly empty houses, Lorenzo tried to remembered what took place the first time he entered Ronda, but found it difficult for some reason. *I feel like I've encountered an anima before, in this place. I don't know how I survived. I feel like there's a missing piece I've misplaced somewhere.* Another scream ruptured through the deep silence of the cursed town. Lorenzo's blood curdled at the demanding sound. *My curse wants my heart back, and there's no one here to save me. Why is my body still running away, when I've already lost?* Thought the traveller, defeated, as his body rushed even faster down a steep street. A great succession of arches gave way to the bridge. Without the protection of the whitewashed houses, he felt naked. No walls impeded him to stare back at the horizon. The light of the dying sun hit especially harsh in that exposed point of the cursed town, and Lorenzo almost felt the rays eroding the ancient stone that held Ronda.

The bridge looks very different when you are standing on it, thought Lorenzo, second guessing the location's safety.

He took the steps that welcomed him into the pavement of the great bridge of Ronda. He studied it in detail. The edges were fortified, giving it the appearance of a castle in between mountains. *How appropriate. I wonder if the builder and his family ever imagined that this would become the last human bastion against the Nothingness,* thought the traveller as he inspected the mastership involved in the structure. Standing over a bench carved into one of the stronghold's walls, Lorenzo carefully peered down to the vertiginous drop. From there he could see almost everything up to the ruined mill; he could see the fire-blackened patch of woods, and the builder retouching his masterpiece atop the precarious scaffolding. Then he looked down to the frozen river. The fall would have definitely finished him- he pictured his body, free falling, cracking when it met the ground. His balance was starting to give in, and his hands were starting to sweat by sheer imagination. Regretting his curiosity, he sat down on the solid bench trying to calm himself. He closed his eyes and looked inward. Only numbness inside of him. No trace of fire. No trace of passion. He had expelled the curse off his body, but it had taken everything as it left, banished from the traveller's body. Nothing else remained. He stood up as he walked down the side path leading to the room within the bridge. The stone steps allowed him to reach one of the inner arches of the bridge, where an unlocked wooden door awaited. Through the entrance, and past a narrow and steep set of steps, he found a simple empty room filled with the builder's tools. A row of mirrors adorned the walls, and a couple of low quality paintings depicted Ronda and its bridge during the history of the place. The vaulted ceiling, made out of the same stone as the rest of the bridge, granted the room a noble quality that was not reflected in its current function.

Lorenzo could almost hear the scream once again. He closed the door behind him, knowing that in there, he would finally open to the curse.

With tears rolling down his cheeks at the realisation, the man did not fight back any longer. He approached the great window in the middle of the bridge's façade. Placing both his hands on the balcony's railing, he looked at the horizon and sighed. The structure's eye was a sentinel observing the End, closer now than ever. The tidal wave rose higher. The stranger looked up at the dying sun as the darkness covered it; so high, that it eclipsed the sun forever. The End had won over the light, and had consumed it in a slithering embrace. Only a dim twilight remained in the realm of Earth.

At least it won't be long now, thought Lorenzo, as a scream filled the room. The high-pitched sound made the windows burst, and as it advanced towards the man, the mirrors covering the room cracked under the cursed vibrations. The floating evil entered the traveller's mouth, slid down his throat, and anchored firmly at his heart. He tasted blood as he entered his nightmare. He had become another victim of the curse. Just like the other villagers of Ronda. Waiting. With just enough time for a last, irrelevant thought.

Soon this space will be too small.

A swallow thought, as it fell asleep.

X - THE CAVE

In which Lorenzo is visited by the past; the writer cries; and everything burns.

Lorenzo was all alone.

So, this is how the curse feels, he thought, as he slowly returned to his body. Even with his eyes closed, he could tell he was not inside the bridge anymore. His throat hurt, clawed and pierced by the curse. His ears rang remembering the unforgiving scream as it entered him. His body resting over something mushy, *somewhere comfortable at last,* he thanked as he moved his hands against the surface that held him. *Damp grass*, he identified. And as he opened his eyes to a starry night, he found himself in the middle of a valley.

It did not take him long to recognise the Sierra that he traversed forever, before he reached Ronda- *and met... Who did I meet? Who am I thinking of?*; no memories, no guilt, no joy.

He knew the mountains around him too well. This time, he knew there was nowhere to travel to, he had finally reached his very own end. He knew he was dreaming, but he also knew that the dream was a nightmare. What his eyes saw was nothing but a tiny snowball, a prison, a mirage. He could feel it.

Standing up slowly, he observed the night sky. The Sun was gone forever. *I still feel nothing*, Lorenzo pointed out, calmly. The dark blue shades of the sky felt like fresh bedding before a Summer night. A gentle breeze moved the endless grass in that little world of his own. *Nowhere to go*. The dotted sky above him shone brightly, spheres of fire observing the lonely man. But there was something else up there, something was not right; he was being observed. Although it was invisible to his eyes, Lorenzo could see the ripples of its movement. It was as if the galaxies and constellations were reflected in a peaceful pond, and something dark and unholy was lurking under the shallows, awaiting its turn to move. The stars trembled as the length of the creature dragged itself around the sky. Lorenzo still felt nothing when he understood that the dream was about to become a nightmare. *This is the curse, as eternal as our existence on Earth. My body is probably still inside the bridge, observing the End approach. A silent carcass who cannot feel much more than I do right now. Repeating the same actions. Caught in an endless loop.* Lorenzo understood well, for in Ronda he couldn't take his eyes off the racing End, ready to destroy everything that existed.

Now he was really far away from his body. In the nightmare, things were just starting for the traveller. The black creature in the sky jumped out from the pond that cloaked it, revealing its shape and details to the lonely Lorenzo. A snake as big as the mountains that surrounded him entered Lorenzo's snow globe. Its scales as black and shiny as polished ebony, but as swift and fluid as petroleum. Pairs of wings, that reminded Lorenzo of bats, divided the body in long sections of pure hunger. Lorenzo did not know where its head or tail was, until the jaws opened. A familiar shrieking sound came out from between the oozing gap. With the scream, it came the rain and with the rain the feelings came back to Lorenzo. The heavy black drops of water tapped his body, soaking him deeper than he imagined.

The traveller and his fear reunited.

The loss and grief filled his cursed soul, like blood spilling over clean water. Lorenzo ran away once more, trying to find shelter somewhere in the fields and mountains around him. The snake screamed again, flying lower and lower, searching for its prey. The traveller ran towards a nearby formation of rocks that announced the beginning of one of the mountains. In the dark, he touched one of the rocky walls and followed it carefully, trying to avoid making any noise. The snake's length was fully inside his nightmare, flying around as a hungry titan. The breeze turned into strong winds, created by the demonic wings getting closer and closer to the scared traveller. Advancing in the middle of the dark, trying to find a thin crack in the stone, his feet failed to find solid ground, and so he fell. The snake continued the hunt.

With the fall came a new feeling; physical pain. From the sounds of rushing water and the humidity in the air, Lorenzo knew he had fallen into one of the many caves populating the Sierra. *These caves have kept people safe from monsters for a long time, please protect me once more,* Lorenzo prayed. *I hope my grandma is not watching from heaven, she would be suffering from seeing me cursed.* The image of her grandma, who he couldn't save from the End, scratched the surface of his numb heart. He handled the hurting thought as a dagger and pushed it deeper into his heart. An open wound. The pain of grief flowed out from the gash, flooding his guts and rising all the way up to his skull, where it found inconsolable relief as tears. 'I miss you so much-' he whispered to himself as he cried, curling up into a ball. The screams from the snake approached his hideout, reminding him of his unavoidable fate. In the darkness of the cave's entrance, silence became thicker. The rain entered the cavity, carried by the occasional gust of wind from the creature's wings. Only the drops and flowing of water filled the intense nothingness in which Lorenzo had found refuge.

From deeper down the cave, a voice rose.

At first Lorenzo thought it could be the murmur of an underground river, or perhaps his own imagination playing tricks on him. But the sound moved, and got closer to where he was hiding. It was a song. *Someone is singing in this nightmare? Wait,* he focused on listening to it over the threatening howls of the snake in the sky. *I know that song, I've heard it before,* remembered the traveller, as his memory took him to church. That was the very song that he heard every Sunday during mass, as his mother professed her love to god. *An all-powerful being that failed to protect humanity from oblivion,* he thought, understanding the irony. Lorenzo mouthed the words in ancient Latin, as he remembered the amount of smacking that took him to learn the hymn. The song paused, and silence filled the cave once more. The familiar smell of church incense reached the cave's entrance.

'Father Leopoldo?' Dared to ask terrified Lorenzo to the emptiness of the hollow, not believing for a second that he would get an answer.

'Shsssh. Let us finish Lorenzo, stop interrupting!' Scolded the old priest, as he proceeded with his tune. The traveller forgot that he was a grown up for a second, as his body remembered the many times he was kicked out of church as a boy. He quickly hid behind a big rock formation; a faint memory, buried deep within his psique, reminded him that he doesn't like meeting lost animas in the dark.

The traveller accepted that in a nightmare, ghosts from the past may be allowed to pay a visit to those they haunt. The Latin words continued to pour from the priest's mouth, in complete darkness. Lorenzo's memories reminded him that the song was about the Mother of god. *Yes, there was this girl in the village; Teresa, who swore she could talk to the Holy Mother. She said this was her favourite song, so Father Leopoldo would sing it every time we gathered. They thought she was holy... I thought she was as bored as I was.*

'Ora pro nobis, sancta Dei Genitrix.'

Sung the profound voice, as it was elevated by the cave walls. It was moving again, slowly approaching Lorenzo.

'Ut digni efficiamur promissionibus Christi,' sentenced the ancient song.

The singing man got so close to him, that the intense smell of incense emanating from the priest's robes made him cough. *Oh no, now he knows exactly where I'm hiding. What is he doing in my nightmare?!* Then silence once again. Lorenzo held his breath, hoping that he wouldn't be discovered. The priest had stopped, and the sound of robes indicated he was looking for something within his holy uniform. Silence once more. Then a sharp sound; a scratching sound, a hiss, that made Lorenzo gasp in horrified anticipation. Before he could understand what was happening, a dim light filled the grotto. He carefully left his hideout and looked at the source of the light, letting his eyes get used to the brightness of the source.

Is that warm light? Is that the light of a match? Slowly, as the head of the stick started to burn and dim, Lorenzo recognised the flame. His memories took him back once again, *the long burning stick is the same one we had in grandma's kitchen, she would light up the fire underneath the big pots of-* His train of thought, interrupted by the sight of the hand holding the matchstick. The hand was not Father Leopoldo's. The silence grew all around Lorenzo, so much that the air pressed against his skin, suffocating him. Darkness hid her features but he knew exactly who that figure was. Another scratching sound, another hiss. Light filled the entrance once again. No more mysteries.

The matchstick approached the face of its holder.

Lorenzo's grandma stood right in front of him.

In a cave of darkness.

In a nightmare.

She looked very tired, like a tree without a drop of sap inside. Consumed, thirsty. Lorenzo couldn't see her face in detail under the burning stick's light, so his imagination filled the gaps. His heart broke looking at her in such a state, and so he jumped towards her, hugging her grandma once again.

'I love you grandma. I'm so sorry!' He repeated as he cried. 'I'm ok. I'm ok. I'm ok.' Repeated his nan trying to comfort him. 'Don't you worry about me Lorenzo, I'm ok!' She said, as she tightened the embrace. Lorenzo released all the pain and sadness and cried. Tears wouldn't stop spilling on his grandma's shoulder. 'Listen my boy. Que I'm ok. Que you don't worry. Que te quiero con toda mi alma, y el alma nunca muere- that's why we're here.' Her calming tone only made him continue crying in loneliness. 'Are you listening, my dear boy? I only want for you to be happy. You have to stand up now.' She gently pushed his body away from the embrace, taking her time to look at her grandson, proudly. 'How could I possibly not know that you love me? You are my boy. My star!' Lorenzo was now looking into her eyes. Her hand kindly removed the tears from his face.

The flying snake screamed once again, bringing Lorenzo back into the reality of the nightmare. The cave shook, vibrating with the high pitched cry. A dark drizzle was being blown into the dark cave by the powerful wings. The grandma looked towards the origin of the sound, protecting the flame of the half consumed match against the wet winds. 'Listen to me, Lorenzo. The matchstick is about to run out. I have no more. You need to walk a bit further down the cave. Inside the deepest darkness there's always some light. Go now, my love.' She stood up, helping him to do the same, and stewarding him towards a path down the cave. The matchstick was almost reaching the grandmother's fingers. Lorenzo was lost for words. The burning smell gave him a sense of comfort amidst all the sorrow.

I am so lonely, he thought as he opened his mouth to share his pain. His nan interrupted him.

'I know, I know. Lorenzo, stop feeling so sorry for yourself.' The traveller turned around, frowning, ready to defend himself. His grandma took his left hand and placed it against the wall. 'Lorenzo, dear boy. There's someone waiting for you at the end of this cave. You are never alone! We're all with you! Go now, go, go!' Before she could finish her sentence, the matchstick's flame reached her fingertips, making her drop it against the wet floor. It went out with a hiss. And with it, Lorenzo's grandmother.

Back in darkness, but not in silence.

The rain was loudly clashing against the stone, and the monstrous titan was getting closer. Lorenzo had to keep on going towards the nightmare's core. With his hand firmly against the wall, and tears streaming down his face, the traveller resumed his journey towards the heart of darkness. He did not allow himself to have one single thought during his descent into the unknown. He knew it was the only thing left to do. The last hiding place for his poor weary bones. Wet feet dragged against the irregular

floor. The left hand scratched by the sharp corners and edges of the uncharted cave.

After a few turns, or at least Lorenzo felt like he was turning, light started to progressively fill the tunnels. *This cannot be. I have only walked downwards, into the stone. This is sunlight... I guess that when you're sleeping anything can happen,* accepted the traveller, as he stood at the heart of the terrible dream. Carved on the rock walls, a window allowed for sunlight to flood the passages. *That window shouldn't be there.* He thought as he shielded his eyes from the piercing sun rays. The song he had heard earlier returned, but instead of Father Leopoldo, it was sung by two voices. The first one, that of a little girl, while the second one belonged to an older woman. Both of them sang different melodies that tangled, answered and triggered each other. He couldn't pin down the origin of the voices, but he knew that there was something sacred taking place, right there, in the depths of the cave.

As his eyes got used to the cascading orange light, he figured out a shape standing by the window. Like his grandma said, there was someone waiting for him at the heart of his fears. He continued walking until he reached the window. *I've seen this view before. I've looked through this window before!*

'Yes, you have,' explained the woman, reading his thoughts. She abandoned the darkness and joined him under the cursed light. 'This is the view from Ronda's Great bridge,' she shared, knowing that the traveller had figured that out already. The wide expanse of bucolic shades of green spilled in every direction, up until the horizon; a simple succession of hills and mountains with no End in sight.

'Is the world not cursed anymore?' He wondered out loud, as the singing voices dimmed down. They were now loud enough to hear them, but quiet enough to wonder if they were being imagined by those who listened.

'Oh, no. It still is.' She turned her face to him, and he noticed she was not much older than him. A thin lady, who looked a bit worn out, stood next to him. The orange light accentuated the shadows over her face. The cheekbones gave her a stern complexion, her eyes told tales of care and understanding. 'This is a window to what it could be. A normal sunset, once again,' her eyes were on him as she spoke.

'What do you need from me? Why is this part of my nightmare?' He asked, as he observed the moving clouds, the flocking swallows hovering far above, swiftly escaping the Winter, and the cream coloured cattle staining the fields below.

'Well. I wish I could give you clear answers, but I don't know much more than you do,' explained the woman as she covered her face, impatient. 'I had a nightmare of my own. I was inside a completely white room. Stuck in bed all day,' the traveller smiled at the thought of such a desirable nightmare. 'Don't smile. I tried to move, to scream, to swallow. I could do nothing other than listening to the sounds that came from underneath my bed. At first I thought they were rats, but then I realised it resembled the sounds of metal against metal.' She gulped before continuing. 'At one point I gathered enough strength to roll over myself and look under the bed. I extended my arm in an incredible effort, when from the darkness beneath, a claw emerged. It was as white as bone, as if they were very long nails. They scratched my forearm, releasing colour into the white room. Red was everywhere.' Lorenzo observed her arms, completely covered by the austere grey dress she was wearing. 'Then the nightmare unravelled. As I was about to be dragged by the white claws into the darkness, I heard a bell. Then the white room disappeared and I felt the floor grow cold and wet. I was in this cave, and this window rose in front of me.' Lorenzo sighed, completely overwhelmed by the amount of dread the world held.

'Do you think we are dead? Do you think this is Hell?' She asked.

'No, I've just seen my grandma. She wouldn't have ended up in Hell.'

'Is she the one singing?'

'No, no clue who that is, sorry', the tune increased its volume, as if the invisible singers were eavesdropping. 'But it's good to know that someone else can hear them singing. I thought I was imagining it'.

'I think losing our sanity should be the last of our worries, in this cave of illusion,' she shivered at a cold breeze that came all the way from the cave's entrance. Crossing her arms over her chest, she revealed, 'I saw someone else before you arrived. This window was a locked door a moment ago. It had a small opening, like a cell. There was someone inside it, and as soon as I touched the lock, it opened. My son was inside. He was the one who said this was a nightmare. *Your* nightmare.'

'Your son? Why is he-' pain filled his heart.

'Yes, he's still alive. The longer we stay here, the closer he gets to the End. I can feel his presence less and less the more he advances towards that terrible beast,' she was trying to remain strong, she had a message to deliver. 'My son said that you need to go and find him, that every being in the world depends on it.'

'Why is your son telling me what to do? And how are we supposed to get out of here?' Said Lorenzo sternly, pointing out at the obvious.

'Lázaro said you should jump.'

'Lázaro!' Exclaimed the traveller at the confirmation of his fear. Inside him, all of his feelings ignited once more.

'Lázaro, Lázaro, Lázaro...' sang the voices hiding in the darkness of the cave. The floodgates containing the traveller's repressed memories, mostly linked to the boy, opened wide and filled his heart to the brim.

He remembered the boy.

He remembered the fear.

'He also said you would be scared, but that I was the one to remind you that this is the perfect opportunity to do things right. To own all of our past and to start becoming who you want to become.' She reached out for the window's handle and opened the french doors easily. A gust of warmer wind entered the cave. Both of them looked at each other trying to figure out what to do next.

'He needs you. He must be close to the End by now. Please, stranger, save my son.' She pleaded, as she pointed her arm at the fall ahead.

The traveller remembered what his nan said, *that I should not feel sorry for myself, that I'm her star.*

The fire within him exploded as a furnace in the peak of Winter. The passion burned so brightly off his skin and clothes, that the corridors in the cave knew darkness no more. Thousands of shadows observed the light, enamoured. They had been hidden in the darkness until the fire in Lorenzo was kindled once again, revealing their shapes, reminding them of their bodies. The voices sang louder, joined by all of Lorenzo's penitent ancestors that gathered in the wet passages of the cave of nightmares. The light projecting from his heart couldn't be contained by the cursed dream, and the purging warmth evaporated every drop of the rotten dark water around them. The light pierced through rock and stone until it spilled outside the cave. The clouds dispersed and the rain stopped. Colour returned to that cursed enclave. The sky opened up to daylight, and the moss covered mountain thanked the bright sunlight coming directly from the traveller's heart. The snake lurking outside seemed to retort and cry at the painful light. Launching its body against the floor and mountains, the monster tried to shake the caves to the ground. Its mighty power succeeded at knocking down tunels and starting landslides. In response, a great earthquake rose from everywhere around them. The little snow globe was on the verge of collapsing.

'Shall we?' Lázaro's mother asked, right before she let her body drop from above the balcony. Lorenzo did not want to look down, just in case his fear gripped his heart with hawk talons once again.

'I'm going to find you, Lázaro!' He shouted, as the noise of the rumbling covered his statement. He placed both his hands on the balcony's railing, looked at the horizon and sighed. Thinking about his grandmother's words, the traveller jumped off the gaping window, and fell into the unknown.

A hawk observing the town of Ronda from above would have seen destruction everywhere; houses fell as if they were made of cards, church bells tolled for the first time since the curse arrived to that corner of the world. The birds who hid in the treetops flew from them, occupying their birthright place in the skies, only to freeze again. The cliffs of the city divided themselves under the shaking pressure, like ancient glaciers giving way to the last drops of heat from a bleeding sun. The Ancient Moorish walls crumbled into piles of rubble. The mines underneath the city disappeared in an instant. The white walls of the old city of Ronda plummeted into rubble and dust. Every area was damaged, but the bridge, which stood proud connecting the town. In the tiny room within it, Lorenzo fell into his body.

He opened his eyes to find the unravelling disaster..

Ronda's cliffs were eating up the city; parks, streets, houses, all fell down with the foundations of the last town on Earth. The monumental bullring was split in half by a gargantuan crack, the orange sand escaping the arena through the fissures on the bedrock. The unluckiest half of the building started its journey towards the bottom of the cliffs, slowly detaching without an obstacle in sight.

The circle was broken.

A half albero sun remained on the ground, as the real one over the horizon tried to emerge from the eclipsing darkness, blinking. Not completely defeated.

Once the rumbling finished, the cliffs of Ronda began at the middle of the bullring.

Only half of the arena stood against the approaching horizon line. Sun-side seats for the destruction of humankind.

And the End was an obsidian bull.

And everyone in Ronda had just become a bullfighter.

XI - THE REUNION

In which three old ladies die; a builder lends a hand; and the traveller travels again.

After a second of profound silence, a haunting chant of pain and harm rose up from every single street in Ronda.

Lorenzo took a moment to feel his body again, wide awake, freed from the curse. He could still feel the warmth of the fire that now consumed him.

Although it didn't show on his clothes and skin, he felt it raging inside, covering every place where fear used to hide with the purest of lights. The stranger was a stranger no more, he had confronted his darkness and obtained an unshakeable truth; he was alive. In fact, when he raised his head to face the End from the bridge's window, he knew he had never been more alive in his entire life. The horizon welcomed him back to cursed Ronda as the ashes started to rain over the last standing village on Earth. The sun was still blinking in desperation, trying to fulfil its original oath, a promise of safety and ligth to humanity and its planet. But the destroying line was too powerful, and all that was left of Earth was a tiny village on top of a few shattering cliffs. As the sun lost its power, observing the cursed circle close tight around Ronda, it sent a final call, a final message. Lorenzo listened carefully.

Son of mine, when the time comes, let your heart be divided. The message from the sun was a riddle that the traveller answered with secret acceptance. He joined his hands into a vessel, as if he was holding the purest of water. Closing his eyes, Lorenzo started to raise his arms until his hands stood between the blinking sun and himself. Forming a cup with his hands, he held the sun. He breathed, feeling the air warmed up air entering his lungs. He opened his eyes as he broke the holding gesture of his hands, opening them until they formed a circle. The base of his palms touched firmly, as his fingertips pushed against each other, arching the fingers into the round shape.

Then, he pointed the flesh spyglass at the horizon, searching for the bleak sun to frame it in the empty space between his hands. Once he found it, he looked at it, and the fire within him met that from the sun.

An ancient gesture from times beyond the past; from times before the moon graced the skies.

As he observed how the sun extinguished, through the lens of his hands, Lorenzo knew he had promised something far beyond his feeble existence. A light-less age had begun, and was set to last way more than humanity's age of light; an eternity of cold twilight. An ominous brightness shone from beyond the End. A single star, a crystal, a bone hanging in space like a pendant, so far away that it was invisible to the human eye. Its power still so terrible and great that it covered the sky with a sense of dusk. Lorenzo, glowing inside the murky bridge, took a deep breath.

'Lázaro, wait, I am coming for you!'

And so, Lorenzo left the little room within the bridge, commencing the long-awaited journey towards Lázaro; towards the End.

The destruction of the little village was worse than Lorenzo had expected. His only way down the cliffs had been destroyed by the rockslides, and his path across the natural slope of the city was now blocked by pure destruction. The screaming wouldn't stop; the cries became so constant that the traveller wondered if that was their new curse. Wherever he ran to, piles of former houses completely obliterated by the quake presented insurmountable obstacles. The desperate calling for help came from underneath too much rubble. So many screams, from so many directions. Lorenzo knew he had to reach Lázaro before it was too late, but the people there needed him. He was alive, he felt the fire, but he was as overwhelmed as he had been since the curse commenced. The loud crying for help from one of the nearby mounds of whitestone and tiles belonged to a little girl. *I have to protect them, I have to save them*, he thought, right before he launched himself on top of the rocks and started removing them bare handed. The more he dug into the mess the larger the stones were, but he continued, feeling every single sharp edge of each stone steadily destroying his hands. The pile of wood beams and rock stained with his own blood, forever, as if he was performing some sort of sacrifice, offering his life as a tribute in exchange for the life of the little one stuck under the rubble.

The rocks were heavy, and he knew his efforts were futile. 'There's no way I'm going to clear all this mess by myself! Stay strong, girl! I'll be back with extra hands to free you from down there, ok?' Lorenzo was desperate to take action, to save everyone. He looked up to the sunless sky and begged the heavens for some help. No answer. Looking around for any signs of human beings he saw the Mondragón palace, still standing as proud as its owners.

'My father, young girl, he's a Mondragón, I will find him and come back with his workers! I'll be here in no time, hold tight!' Lorenzo shouted through the openings between the piling rocks. Then he turned around quickly, trying not to trip with the many rocks he had removed. His hands were still dripping red. As his feet reached solid ground, his body crashed against someone. The builder's hefty body stood there, in front of him, covered in ashes and with a mouth full of blood.

'Thank god I am not scared of heights, that was a nasty fall! Ha! Go find the landlord, boy. Maybe this will be the time when he repays all of his debt to this city of cliffs. I'll take care of the little girl.' In understanding, Lorenzo nodded and ran towards the palacio Mondragón, praying for his father's improbable help.

He was on the move again, dodging all sorts of debris, when three immobile lumps of black fabric in the middle of the way brought the wanderer to a halt. That part of the street had never been so silent, not even the cries for help of the people of Ronda dared to invade it. A place that had been filled with constant laughter for the duration of the curse, could hardly become a place for sorrow. He kneeled down, tears in his eyes, 'Ladies! Are you awake!? Ladies please, tell me you're still in the world of the living!' Voiced Lorenzo as he carefully uncovered the bodies of Maria, Eustaquia and Perpetua. Their houses were destroyed, but as they were outside, they didn't get the worst of it. Lorenzo feared the commotion would have been too much for their ancient hearts. *They look so peaceful*, he thought, remembering his grandma's hands around the matchstick.

The traveller took a deep breath and wondered out loud, 'After all, making the jump into the End may have been an act of kindness.' And holding Eustaquia's body, he thought of Lázaro.

'Oh my, Sister-Angela-of-the-Cross-Guerrero-y-Gonzalez-may-she-be-blessed-in-the-skies! That was a bang so loud that even I could hear it! And the lord knows I've been deaf since I was thirty!' Said Eustaquia waking up from her slumber in Lorenzo's arms, as she broke into laughter. Maria raised from the floor, holding her head, readjusting it into her body. Followed by Perpetua, who tried to tidy up herself, keeping it together. Both of them joined the laughter, cackling like they always did. The traveller was so relieved he could have cried, alas he had no energy to spare. They were alive and fine, there were plenty who weren't and they needed his help.

'Virgin Mary and all the Saints in heaven! Thank god we weren't inside the houses!' Said Maria, stood up and ready to work, while checking the horrible destruction around them. Inspecting the rubble, Maria found a small statue of the Archangel Michael defeating the serpent, she dusted it and placed it on top of a flat rock in the pile. The traveller looked at them in awe, wishing he was that fundamentally fearless. The three ladies muttered a prayer in unison. Once they finished, Perpetua cleared her voice as she addressed all of them, 'Thank god my husband died in his sleep years ago, while I was ironing... Otherwise he'd be part of that pile of dust. Blessed be the Holy Spirit for keeping us well and together. Now, get up and ready my dear friends, we have a big mess in our hands and it looks like we're going to be cleaning for the rest of our lives!' The three of them were laughing so hard in agreement that they started coughing amidst all the ash and dust. As the ladies armed themselves with their brooms to organise their corner of the village, Lorenzo understood they would be safe and continued his journey to request help from his father.

The traveller was running towards the palace when he saw an old greyhound barking, by himself, looking for its owner. It scratched the remnants of a wooden door, biting and pulling from a ball of yarn stuck underneath the mess. Sadly, Lorenzo could tell the silence around those piles indicated that the dog wouldn't be lucky on this occasion. Almost at his destination, he kept running. His strides echoed as he entered the tiny square where the regal home awaited his illegitimate heir. The buildings around that area were mostly untouched, with only a couple of the highest towers succumbing to the tremors. The Mondragón's fortress stood hurt, with one of its steeples blocking the service entrance. *I need to hurry, I'm not sure for how long Lázaro will be with us,* he rushed himself as he started walking towards the main gate. As he was about to cross the palace's main entrance, a slender figure jumped on him, restraining him. The traveller forcefully released himself from the weak grip, turning around to find his aggressor's identity.

Lázaro's mum stood in front of him, pale and ill, wearing only her humble nightgown.

The ashes were starting to build up into a thin layer of ungrateful snow.

'I told you- to go find Lázaro- what are you doing here?' The illness still affected her breathing. Her shiny skin denoted a light fever.

'I need to talk to my father, there's people who need help out there. My father can help!' He explained, becoming aware of his bad decision.

'I don't think there's- much more time left.' She breathed out her words, wheezing heavily as she found respite by leaning against one of the marble columns adorning the patio. 'We need Lázaro back, and more importantly- he needs you.' She coughed as Lorenzo clenched his jaw in a proud and stern expression. 'Listen, traveller! Are you listening?' She raised her voice, as she pointed with a porcelain finger right towards Lorenzo's heart. 'My boy hasn't met the End yet- I can feel him!' The fire inside Lorenzo's heart danced at the thought of reuniting with Lázaro. He didn't have to be alone. Lázaro was alive. Looking around they could feel Ronda, a wounded beast, protecting its children with the last drops of its strength. The End was close, but hope was closer.

'Go traveller! Travel once again! Find my Lázaro- I will take care of your father- I know him well.' Lorenzo didn't respond, because he knew that she was right. He knew what he had to do, to take action, to save Lázaro.

'He needs you right now- go now! Go!' She pushed him outside of the palace, exorcising his presence from the haunted building, as if he had been a wandering ghost until that very moment. 'Do what you were born to do- run away like your life depends on it!' She stabbed him with words. Spurring on a horse.

And the horse bolted.

Turning his back to his family once again, Lorenzo ran as if he was a gust of wind sailing over the angriest of seas.

Lázaro perched at the very edge of the world. The ground beneath his feet, almost transparent. The ashes of a world destined to be consumed rose everywhere around the boy; he could hardly open his eyes. What the blackness ahead was, still remained a mystery.

He was ready to jump.

The Seer observed the boy from afar, curious about the boy's fate that she had envisioned. In preparation for the moment in which the world's last hope was finally consumed, the rain of ashes paused. Lázaro resisted at the very edge of his fears. The boy felt the power of the all-destroying wall pushing against him, trying to play with him on its own terms. Wanting him to fight back, to run away. Lázaro was ready to conquer this last battleground, and so, he kept on pushing against the membrane of death, walking blindly through the disappearing world. Through the resistance, through the thick air of oblivion, the decision was made; he would jump.

Lázaro forced himself into the deadliest of embraces, a snake devouring itself from the tail, that destroyed everything in the process. He was scared no more, he knew what he had to do. As the End rushed through the fields of Ronda, the wind tried to escape by creating whirlwinds and gusts that in turn slowed the boy's advance. Still, he walked firmly, shielding his eyes from the specs of the life that had fallen to the End. A black bull, rabidly bringing nothingness into the last remaining kingdom of humanity. The remaining light in the sunless sky seemed to dim even more, this close to the End.

This is not Death, for Death is still something. This is pure Nothing. Lázaro thought, right before he took a step that met no ground. The last step before encountering the raging silence of the End.

And the mystery only grew louder.

Behind the terrible curtain of destruction and ashes, of

a world that once was, existed nothing but the deepest darkness the boy had ever seen. Time worked differently in that thick realm, and his body entered it very slowly. His right leg and head were past the End, as his left hand slowly followed, failing to hold onto the Nothing that surrounded him. In between the fear and regret the young one was feeling, he allowed himself to enjoy time passing again, even if it was that slowly. He enjoyed every millisecond as if it was a day, after being completely frozen for so long; a fish returning to the ocean, breathing once again. A puppet whose strings had been cut; no more movement as his body disconnected from his mind, slowly turning as transparent and fragile as glass. Shattering slowly. The embrace of the nothingness brought him a memory, *I've been here before. Oh, how I've missed the night.* Lázaro thought, shutting his eyes. Sudden lightning struck his body; no light, no sound, but his body raptured as his senses heightened. Slowly entering the End, he understood that he was transcending into something higher. He was returning somewhere deeper, where he could not be his individual self anymore. He wasn't himself, but everyone. Nothing existed, so everything was possible.

There's always something after an ending, something that stays with you and connects you to the collective living. Nothingness was only the Beginning. The boy understood as his body continued crossing the End's veil of oblivion, and its fleshy boundaries blurred into the unknown realm. His left arm was inside, only his right arm and foot remaining on Earth. He was about to be completely obliterated. Forgotten.

Lázaro couldn't see it properly, but he knew something else was in there. He heard a call. A single dimminute star shone lonely in the middle of what-was-not, and it was calling him into the light. A spiral of golden dust marked the way, and the star waited. For just a second, the young one felt the eye of an evil presence scrutinising every single aspect of his existence. As Lázaro stopped being, he felt like he was drinking water after surviving a desert.

Like sleeping after many lives of being awake.

He was ready to go; he was happy to let go.

'This is the End.' The announcement vibrated across the limits of the boy's ethereal body. A sound that was many, a choir of voices that belonged to every single person who had succumbed to the evil darkness. Lázaro got ready to start his journey towards the far away star, where a vengeful ancient god patiently sat in its throne. He knew he had to join the light. He had to join the pilgrimage towards the shining star where nothing else existed. He had to sacrifice the very nature of his consciousness and give way to an age of emptiness. Both his arms had crossed the veil, and his whole body commenced to disappear, falling in slow movement.

I am flying towards the light now. I am finally free. The transcending boy felt, as he noticed his body moving millimetre by millimetre, closer to the reason why the End existed.

And he left.

His body stopped moving forward. The call from the star grew louder, firmer. Commanding him to advance. Still, his body wouldn't move. Someone else's hand was crossing the dark limit, and gripped Lázaro's left hand strongly. Lázaro intended to turn around, to release himself from the earthly grip. Alas, time flowed so slowly. The arm started pulling Lázaro into the world of the living.

'No! I can't go back! How could I exist if I am not myself anymore. I am not one but all. I have seen the Star behind the End! I cannot go back through the veil!' The boy screamed inside his mind, as the outsider's arm pulled him closer to the world of the living without hesitation. The boy's ghostly body retracted its path as it started to cross once more the thin layer of glutony. Looking in the direction of the Star one last time, he saw fury. The hungry being sat on its throne shrieked in anger. The completion of their revenge would have to take a little bit longer.

And so, a swallow returned to a golden room.

XII - THE SHOOTING STARS

In which Lorenzo is late; the End is touched, a hawk surveys the land; and a hero is put to rest.

Lorenzo had arrived too late, Lázaro was already going through the End. Suppressing his terror of the evil horizon, he sprinted with all his might and grabbed the boy's hand by its fingers, at the very moment when they were about to disappear through the dark veil. The traveller tried in vain to get hold of more of the boy's hand, while he avidly avoided touching the terrible End. The wind felt electric as it was sucked into the void of nothingness. The horizon raged into another earthquake as it hurried its advance, trying to devour the remaining flesh of Lázaro at once. Lorenzo was losing the final battle. He could feel the thick invisible veil trying to break past his feet and legs. This was his end as much as it was his friend's. His sweaty hands, from running without stopping to catch a breath, were giving up. The fingers slipped through his grip. Lorenzo fell backwards on his back, and saw the boy's hand continuing to disappear right in front of him.

Two old hands appeared from behind Lorenzo, who saw a bunch of colourful fabrics moving quickly towards the End. The woman providing the helping hand had put her arm right through the veil, without hesitation. She grabbed Lázaro's hand and pulled, returning part of it back into their realm. Her both bony hands anchored the boy's remaining flesh, using her whole body weight to counter the pull from the End. Lorenzo looked at her in awe. *Right when everything seemed lost, this lady appeared out of nowhere and -* He was quickly interrupted by urgent hand gestures.

'You! Wanderer! What the heck were you doing? You are so much later than I expected!' She grunted from the effort. Lorenzo stared at her, taking a second to realise that her strength was about to fail against the End. He stood up quickly and got closer to the woman not really knowing how to help.

'Stop staring and do something! This is not happening like I foretold. This is not what I saw in the creases of his palm! I am not supposed to be saving Lázaro, you are!'

She indicated with her head in the direction of the boy, as Lorenzo tried to figure out the best way to take over her. Their hands swapped. Lorenzo's grip was firmer this time, and so he started to pull with all his might.

'That's it, young man. Pull!'

The End shook the ground once more, as Lorenzo continued to play a game of tug against the final boundary on Earth. The boy was the rope. His face showed the effort that required returning from the place where everything ends. The Seer embraced his waist from behind him, and joined her strength to Lorenzo's. The boy's arm started to appear from across the empty wall. Lorenzo found it easier to pull as the boy returned to his rightful realm, and slowly, a limb at a time, the two of them released Lázaro's body from the claws of nothingness. The Seer heard a scream of desperation that came from inside the End.

'May we be spared from succumbing to their ruling,' she muttered as a prayer to dispel the frustration emanating from the other side.

The wind around the End seemed to celebrate the small victory prematurely, but as Lorenzo grabbed the damaged boy, he realised that Lázaro was not breathing.

The End rumbled once again and advanced, eager to claim what he had already conquered. Lorenzo moved quickly to avoid getting dragged past the boundary, carrying the boy with the help of the Seer.

Lorenzo ran a few metres away from the final horizon, and laid the boy down against the dried up earth.

'Lázaro! Lázaro! Wake up! I can't believe I made it on time!' Lorenzo shouted at the inert body, while embracing the boy. The traveller observed Lázaro as his eyes filled with tears. His friend was turning into a ghost, like made out of glass; transparent and fragile; inexistent. The boy was back, but Lorenzo knew he wasn't really there. 'You have to wake up my friend, please! Your mum told me there was time. She said you're our last hope! Please Lazarillo, wake up!' The boy was not reacting to the desperate plea, wearing an expression of pain, He had seen through the End. The Seer was catching up with herself, her back was not what it used to be, and the unexpected exercise was making her every bone ache. After gently stretching for a second, she approached the two men.

'Don't wake him up yet, for he has seen what lies behind the End, my love. He would go crazy, our poor lad.' The Seer adjusted her many layers of precious fabric while staring into Lorenzo's soul. 'As much as Lázaro has seen past the darkness, the darkness has seen past Lázaro. They are one now, and the nothingness won't let go.'

'There must be something we can do!'

'This is as far as the story goes, I cannot see past this very point.'

'What do you mean? Who are you?'

'Lorenzo, I am a seer, I was supposed to help Lázaro. I'm afraid we've both failed.' She kneeled down next to them and extended her hands to touch the boy's chest. Her hands went right through Lázaro's ethereal presence. What once was a land full of life and nature, was now a desolate wasteland where only hollow trees and a fractured ground remained. The End remained unstoppable, and the lost light that was left started to leak through it. Darkness grew all around them.

'I failed again. I was stupid for thinking there was some

hope left in this world.' Lamented Lorenzo, as almost the whole of his friend became transparent. His glass body slowly divided into countless ashes floating in the raging winds. The slithery obsidian end line was advancing towards them silently. Knowing its own victory, the End sent a clear sign to the last remnants of the world; a sound so deep and terrifying that the Earth trembled deeper than before. A horn. An indication that with Lázaro, hope had departed the land of Ronda. The last remaining bastion of humanity. The traveller looked at the Seer as she stared right through the evil mantle, as if she could see what took place behind it. The horn was blown once more.

Nearby, a forgotten washing line consisting of two poles and a string, waved manically its white drapes to the winds as it was swallowed by the End.

'Unless...' The Seer took a second. She had just understood what her fate was. 'The End is blind, it has no eyes. Only hunger!'

'Please tell me that you know how to help Lázaro.' Begged Lorenzo, without an ounce of energy inside his body, as light disappeared from the world.

'I have always known. I have always been aware. I must admit, it is quite refreshing not having a clue of what happens next.' She said almost whispering, as she looked at the vanishing body of the boy. 'The End has tasted a human soul, and only a human soul will suffice.' The Seer finished, puzzling Lorenzo. But before he could ask a single question, the lady ran and jumped into the dark cloak of destruction separating reality and the unknown. Exchanging her life for that of the boy, she met the End. Lorenzo tried to follow her, to grab her, to avoid another soul to be consumed by the cursed storm. He was too late once again. He didn't have one drop of energy left within him, not a teardrop to spare in that barren land. *Why did you do that, crazy woman?* He thought as he turned around to witness his friend vanishing.

But Lázaro became visible and solid once again, peacefully resting his body against the ground. Lorenzo threw himself at the boy, touching his face, making sure that he was breathing and well; that he was not dreaming nor cursed. He used his hands to brush away the ashes from the other side of the End piling over the returned Lázaro. Then he understood what the Seer had done. *A sacrifice,* Lorenzo admired, as if the lady had sent a message directly to his heart. A shooting star crossed the twilight sky towards Ronda, and light regained some strength in the realm of the living. The flame of hope within him ignited once again, and this time he would set everything on fire if he had to for Ronda to remain safe.

The final night was closer than ever, and the End emitted the terrifying horn sound once again. Now being able to firmly grab Lázaro, the traveller didn't think twice and ran away from the black velvet mouth of the boundary. He followed the direction of the shooting star, and kept going until he reached the first ruined mill. There, he laid down the boy, took some water from the still river and poured it over the young one's face.

'I can't believe the lady jumped through the End! I can't believe you almost went through it! Please wake up my friend, we have lots to do. Ronda needs us.' Lorenzo couldn't wait for the boy's eyes to open again. 'Without you, everything is over.' He sat next to Lázaro and closed his eyes, allowing himself to observe the ball of fire that grew inside his chest. Trying to understand what it required to stay burning. He knew Lázaro would return in time, so he waited.

Not long had passed until Lázaro started to slowly open his eyes. Regaining consciousness, pain was the first thing the boy felt. Not any pain, but an extortionate amount of sorrow. Voices piled inside his mind, not letting him use his senses to see the world around him. Everything left alive on Earth was talking to him, sending secret messages just for him. Those weren't just words, they were feelings, sensations and visions that played right before his eyes. The overwhelmed body convulsed under the amount of information filling his brain.

He disconnected his mind from his physical body in order to survive the transition. He sent his consciousness above his body, just like the trees had done before they encountered the witch. He still observed the scene; his body laying down, and Lorenzo tenderly consoling him through his trance.

'Boy, stay with me, breathe again. Your mother will be so proud of you.'

Heard Lázaro from the heights. *I know that she is proud. I can actually feel her pride right now.* The world around him flickered, the forests and paths expanded in distorted scales, he couldn't see himself or Lorenzo anymore, just his mother appeared in front of him, like a phantom, taking some of the villagers of Ronda towards the remaining half of the bullring. Another distortion of space and time, and he was back at the miserable view of his own suffering body. *My breath is not regular, my body may not make it. I need to understand. I need to open my heart to knowledge, to feelings.* Above him, a hawk glided perpetually, stuck in the curse and waiting for the End to claim her. Without knowing how, his awareness stretched in shape, and pierced the hawk mid flight. His eyes were not his anymore. He was the hawk.

From inside his new bird body, he observed the land beneath him in a way he couldn't have imagined before.

Every tree, every branch, every stone, every animal, every human - all the connections between them naked in front of him. A spider's web of neon green patterns, everchanging, disconnecting and reconnecting as they followed the sacred pattern of the planet. He gained the knowledge he needed to understand his new status; his human body was also part of that network, and his perception was now free from the human blocks that rendered them blind. *For the first time in my life, I can now see.* After coming back from the End, he wasn't one anymore, but all of them. He was connected. And not just to present time, but all of the memories of the creatures of Ronda were his. He saw the first celtic tribes arriving to the mines, the foundations of the Great Bridge being laid, he saw his father leaving, and back to present times, he saw his mother gathering everyone at the half Bullring. He saw the curse commencing when an adventurous cat came across the meteorite that contained an ancient god's revenge, a terrible being who had been banished from Earth a long time ago; during a time that our history books cannot reach. A time so lost in the past, that it is closer to the future than it is to our present.

The boy kept searching through the timeline of his awareness, when he turned his inner eye inwards. Lázaro encountered a mist that, when dispelled, discovered memories of what could take place next. Memories from possible futures that he observed carefully. The awakened boy was cautious, *should I go too far into what's to come, the good and the bad? I may get lost in a web of overwhelming despair and joy.* But Ronda needed his new vision more than ever, so he kept drifting through the mist, towards the culmination of the End's journey. The available pathways kept disappearing in front of him, the more ground the End covered, the less options left for the living.

After swift consideration of all the possible outcomes, he understood what he had to do next. The only potential path that he could follow to win over the End expanded in front of him. *Difficult, yes, but not impossible. I am the embodiment of Time. Time is held within my body.*

As soon as Lázaro understood his new identity, the hawk escaped the curse and flew freely across the sky. Time was back in the realm of the living, however, the boy could still sense the curse, deeply ingrown inside most of the villagers of Ronda. He could now notice the little variations in the connections between creatures; when something was cursed, the green colour became shades of grey and white. The cursed were asleep. Their souls tangled in their bodies, unable to leave their physical manifestations, condemned to being immutable, a repetition. A destiny worse than death. Timeless. Traversing through the mist of future one last time, following every branching fork ahead of him, Lázaro convinced himself of the steps to follow. Once ready, he descended, returning to his body.

'Swallows...' Lázaro mumbled as he regained consciousness and battled the sharp headache he suffered. Lorenzo's face focused in front of his eyes.

'Lazarillo! Oh boy, that was close!' The traveller exclaimed in celebration. 'A weird old lady said some crazy stuff about you, I didn't get a word. Next thing I know she was running towards...' Lorenzo overshared, excited to be once again with his fellow adventurer. 'I think she did it

so we- I think she actually-' Lorenzo tried to articulate his
thoughts to the kid, not knowing what Lázaro was going
through. The pain of the suffering people, in the land
surrounded by the End, reunited inside his chest.

'I know what she did, my good friend Lorenzo. She gave
us one last hope, and we shall not waste it. Now, Lorenzo,
we have work to do. Let's wake up the sleeping ones.' Said
the boy as he was trying to calibrate his newly gained
awareness, while leaning on the traveller to stand up.
Both of them allowed themselves a second to breathe,
and although Lorenzo couldn't understand what his
friend was going through, he knew Lázaro was different
now. There was a certain difference in the way gravity
felt around the boy; it felt as if he was navigating his way
through a crowded room.

Ronda was slowly covered by an nightime of evil, but now
Lázaro knew better. He didn't need light to see any more,
for he could see through every single eye remaining in the
lands of Ronda. Directing his vision towards the forest,
Time commanded light. A string of blue will-o-wisps lit
the way. The path to follow was clear.

'Follow my lead dear Lorenzo, do not trip or waste one second of precious time. If you do, it will be one second too late.' Said the boy as he started walking towards the city atop the cliffs.

'While you were away a horrible earthquake destroyed the city. People are suffering. Many have died.' Lorenzo broke the news.

'I know, my dear friend. I feel every single one of them. I feel their suffering.' The pair walked swiftly, accompanied by the blue light of the playful flames. 'I've got a plan, I'm not sure if it will work, but we need to try it. We need to gather every single one of them in the bullring, if we want to have a chance against the End.' Said Lázaro, without a drop of hesitation in his voice.

'Will we be able to save them all?' As soon as the traveller asked that question, he feared he may not be ready for the answer. He was as confused as he had been since the beginning of their journey. *His walk is different. His voice is different. But when I look at him, I can only feel hope. I don't fully understand what has taken over him, but I'm willing to do whatever it takes to win against the End.* He followed the steps of the new Lázaro, a bit creeped out by the dancing tongues of fire marking their route. *Last time they showed up, it didn't end up well for us.*

The blue halo that came from the friendly fire, covered the landscapes they traversed, reflecting all over Lázaro. His skin was still translucid after his crossing of the End, and as the boy looked back at Lorenzo to answer his question, the traveller could see the changes in his face. *His eyes are completely white!* Observed Lorenzo in fear, only to realise that his eyes were still there, they were just more transparent than the rest of his body. A reminder that his friend was still an apparition, a ghost haunting the world's end.

'Think of all the humans who have succumbed to the End already; my father, your family, complete countries, continents, everything you can imagine outside of this very last town. We have only one chance to bring all of them back. So stay alert my dear friend.'

Lázaro wisely explained, as Lorenzo felt as if he was punched in the stomach by the boy's demolishing truth-saying. The traveller could hardly hold back his emotions at the thought of all who had perished.

Snapping out of his sadness, he responded, 'I am terribly saddened by their loss, but with you by our side, it is time to fight back. I won't be distracted by my own feelings and I'll be ready to do as I must, Lázaro.' He pleaded.

'We will do what we can do; no more, no less. Our best. Whatever happens after that, I'm afraid it is not for us to judge.' Concluded the boy, as they reached the burning forest. Lorenzo agreed.

The flames had spread across the trees very quickly. The blue tint became a fiery glare of red and black. Time was back in the land, so there was no barrier that impeded fire to break through bark and leaves. Trees fell all around them, twisting and breaking. Exploding trunks propelled dust and wood chips all over the air. Lázaro looked up, observing the fire raging over them, crowning the trees of rubies and amber. He felt the trees deep within him. They were rejoicing in the sacred union with fire. Transforming. Moving on.

Lázaro also felt the trees' curiosity towards the little

human. All the trees connected beneath their feet. Lázaro
kneeled by a tree stump that had already been consumed
by fire, the coals still burning deep inside, and touched
the squirming protruding roots.

The hum took over their skulls once again; the boy
listened.

We have been burning but never burnt. Now we are dying.
Now, in our sacrifice, we can extinguish this fire. Now
we can commence to grow again, as we've done millions
of times before. The same way you've transceded your
humanity, we will transced our roots.

Lázaro knew there was something they had to do in the
forest. Something mandatory, if they wanted to reach the
future where they prevailed over the End.

'Please, dear trees, take me to her.' He whispered to the
roots of the dying stump, as he closed his eyes, leaving
Lorenzo puzzled. The green network of living beings
became visible to his mind's eye, as he followed the
pulse of the burnt out stump towards his goal. Standing
up, with his eyes still closed, the boy followed the trees'
directions, slowly navigating through a sea of fire.

Whenever the boy reached a burning trunk, the fire extinguished, leaving only a mess of coal and darkness. After a tree was redeemed in fire, it would direct the boy through another pulse of the green network, pure life, indicating the next stop in his pilgrimage. He continued to walk, following the web of beings. The traveller followed him closely. *How can he tell where he is going? His eyes are closed!*

He continued to extinguish the fire, talking to them in whispers, letting them know that the time for their regrowth would come soon. He reached the end of the path and opened his eyes. A pile of leaves appeared in front of him, untouched. The leaves were dry, as if Autumn had taken over that little clear in the middle of the forest. Unnatural, as everything around them was. Lázaro felt someone buried below the leaves, so he kneeled once again and leaned over the leafage. The orange pile reacted by moving away from the boy, responding to his proximity, discovering the mystery they were hiding. Underneath, the naked body of the witch who summoned fire struggled to breathe properly. She had been burnt badly, and with Time back in the realm, her body had started to decay. Her dark eyes were lost, not being able to acknowledge the boy in front of her. The witch had tried everything within her power to dispel the curse and bring back time to the land of Ronda. Now Time itself kneeled over her, and carefully placed his left hand over her forehead. Her ribs moved without rhythm. At the touch, the witch screamed, like a cornered wild animal. Lázaro shushed her, 'You have done what you had to do for us to be here. For that, I thank you.' He was not scared of witches anymore. So he whispered, 'You contained the curse by yourself for millenia. You don't have to fight back any more, you are free to move on.' The witch listened and exhaled deeply, letting her earthly body die.

Lorenzo quickly approached the site, alarmed at the wail. But he did not find the naked, burnt mess of skin and hair that the boy saw under the pile of Autumn leaves. He discovered Lázaro kneeling next to a queen. A regal figure that wore clothes washed by the purest green and blue he had ever seen. The gold decorations that covered the garment left them both in awe. Her expression, with her eyes now closed, seemed to be peaceful at last. Her skin glistened from the inside, as the body disappeared slowly. The dark trunks pointed up above, as another shooting star raced across the sky to meet the End.

'We couldn't save her, Lázaro, is this ok?' The traveller asked, surprised as always of being in the presence of the occult.

'Like me, she had seen what lies after the End. She is safe now.' He explained to a distressed Lorenzo.

'Who was she? Did you know her?'

'She was a Moorish Queen who ruled Ronda ages ago. She was also the witch who tried to bring back Time by burning the realm.' Continued the boy. 'The Queen was there when the curse first came to this world, a lethal present from the ancient power sitting behind the End. Her husband, the King, accepted the present in all his greed - she couldn't stop him and his followers from opening it. She tried, my friend, I promise you she did. The temptation of controlling Time was too much for the weak hearts of empty men. As the curse revealed

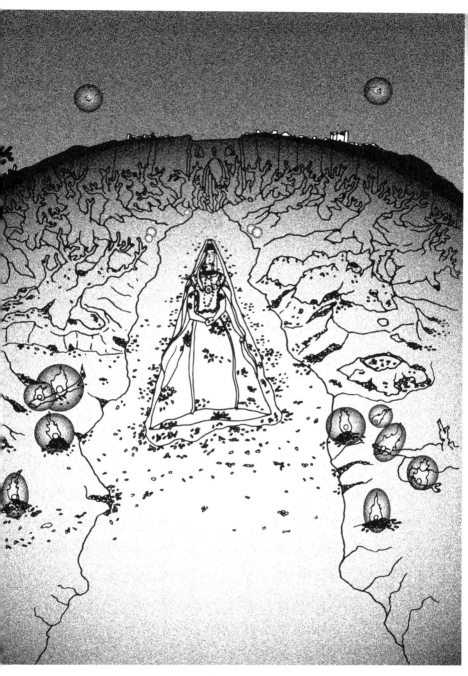

itself, she had to kill him with her own hands. She embraced the curse and contained it in the deepest, most secluded area underneath the cliffs of Ronda, where she would mourn forever, cursed. Underneath what would eventually become the bullring. She shielded us all at the cost of her own life becoming timeless. We owe her the very existence of humanity, Lorenzo.' Shared the boy as he saw the past flash in front of his eyes, shivering at the meteorite parting the sky, and at a little shadow undoing the Queen's shielding spell.

Lázaro stood up as he took a second to admire the confused expression of his friend. Holding his hand, he pulled Lorenzo and continued walking.

XII 1/2 - THE PROCESSION

In which Lázaro's cheek turns red; good gossip is shared; and a man is left behind.

The vengeful god pushed its all-devouring horizon in careless rage. The pace of the destruction became vertiginous, an unstoppable avalanche. By the time the small company was walking into the village, the End had swallowed the abandoned mills and most of the river. And the rumbling became more frequent, although by then, most things susceptible of collapsing were already shapeless piles of rubble. The party climbed the cliffs of Ronda, using Lázaro's vision to discover newly created passages and avoiding any roadblock. They moved upwards without hesitation under the protection of the stoic bridge - the scaffolding was completely destroyed, but the construction remained untouched. *You should be proud, builder. You made her well.* Thought Lorenzo as he tried to follow the boy's precise steps.

Further past the cliffs, the bullring welcomed the inhabitants of Ronda for one last fight. Only a small strip of calcined woods separated Ronda from its conclusion. The rain of ashes became stronger as the final chapter approached.

They took a moment to look back and see all that was left.

'Can you tell me what it is? What do we have to do to win?' Asked Lorenzo, not being able to control his need to know more about what was about to happen.

'I can't, my dear friend. If you knew, the only thing that could save us wouldn't take place.' Muttered Lázaro mysteriously. 'You will have to believe in me, and in everything that the End has taught you so far.' Then he turned around and kept on walking. He was needed somewhere else. Lorenzo accepted the mystery and followed the boy into the Old Town of Ronda, praying that when the time came, he would be brave enough to help.

It didn't take them long until Lázaro reached the three old ladies. They were standing in the middle of the street, looking upwards to the sky, so still that they could have been statues. Around the three figures, who held tightly their three brooms, twenty piles of dust were neatly arranged. The piles belonged to their former houses, which

271

were now gone. The tiny statue of the Archangel Michael continued to preside over the scene, balancing itself on top of a pillar, part of the ruins. *Even at the end of the world, they have been tidying around. They are unstoppable,* thought Lorenzo, marvelling at the sheer resilience of the women. *They had brushed the whole street!* That was at least, until the ashes started falling.

As Lázaro approached Perpetua, she said, 'Today we're having the most peculiar weather! Do you know that saying? The one for when a day ends with a beautiful orange sunset? The Virgin Mary must be ironing in heaven and all that! Well, she definitely left the iron on and has burnt something!" The lady gestured dramatically to the sky, then pointing out at the raining ashes that had started to mix with their perfectly organised street. The three of them laughed, but so softly, that Lorenzo gathered that the women were really tired, *which means time is getting to them. The cursed people are trying to wake up.*

'Now we have to start from the beginning. All the hard work for nothing!' María lamented.

'It's getting late, and colder. This Winter is going to be a bad one. Oh how I wish I had my Oneferio with me, so he could heat my bed!' Said Eustaquia, trying to cheer up the other two. They were so exhausted, that for the first time since the curse started, they couldn't find the strength to laugh.

The boy moved closer, touched by the attitude of the three women. They had spent an eternity together, and only now he could understand what they were going through. *They are fighting the curse with laughter, that's all they have been doing from the moment the curse arrived. Trapped in a nightmare of their own and still being light and cheerful.* He walked towards Perpetua, unnoticed, as they were too focussed on the messy layer covering the pavement. Getting closer, Lázaro graced Perpetua's cheek and planted an innocent kiss on it. He did it with all the care that his body contained.

'Lazarillo...' She muttered in complete shock, as she looked everywhere around her. She was a newborn baby, curiously observing the world around her as if she had been somewhere completely different for her whole existence.

The other two ladies remained cursed, dutifully tidying

their pebbles and their corners. The boy approached Eustaquia, who took a second to rest, leaning on her broomstick. Lázaro gently rubbed her back, and hugged her from the side.

'Eustaquia, my friend, it's time to wake up.' He whispered, invoking all the care his mother ever gave him.

'No. It cannot be.' She said, placing her hands over her head in horror. As she took in the destruction around her, the broomstick hit the ground with a loud bang.

Maria looked in the direction of the sound, startled, when she saw Lázaro moving towards her. He was smiling. She was terrified. She didn't want to see the world as it was. She wanted to remain cursed. Walking backwards, she tried to avoid his waking touch.

'No. No. I don't want to. No, please. No.' Maria begged as the boy got closer.

'Trust me María, we all need to be here. We all need you, so we can see the sunrise once again.' Lázaro explained, extending his arms. Scared to death, she hid herself in the depths of her black shawl. The boy reached her and put her arms around her with all the care that was left on Earth, as the woman sobbed between his arms. Lorenzo observed his friend's new vision with pride, but also fear of what was to come. Turning his head to the left, the End had almost eaten up most of the forest. *I don't know what it is that could save us from this horror.*

As Lázaro hugged María, the arms of the other two ladies joined in the healing embrace. Understanding everything, the three ladies cried. Lorenzo walked closer to them, too embarrassed to join the display of affection. Instead, he remained at a safe distance and placed a comforting hand on top of one of the ladies.

After a moment of quiet sobbing, Maria's head popped out from the mesh of shawls and flesh, 'Lázaro! My dear, dear, boy! What's happened to Ronda?' Her voice was as shaky as her legs were.

Breaking the moment of peace, Eustaquia joined, 'Where are our houses? Where are our houses, boy? Why has God forsaken us!?'

Perpetua sat down with effort and pulled her hair dramatically, 'I can't understand. When did all this happen? Tell me I am dreaming!' The three of them cried, losing control over their emotions. Reality was simply too much for their hearts.

Lázaro held Maria's hand and asked them, 'Please ladies, join hands together,' his voice did not belong to a child anymore, and what he commanded, they did. 'The pain will pass. Don't fight it, find a way of holding onto it for the rest of our adventure. We will find a couple more people between all this mess and then we will join everyone at the bullring. That place will keep us safe... for now.' The young one talked with authority and kindness. As they held hands in a circle, the flame in the boy's heart travelled and kindled sibling fires inside each one of the old ladies. As their bodies warmed up, their despair allowed for a nervous calm.

After a short silence of reflection, María spoke, 'Yes Lazarillo, we'll follow you. Please guide us to safety.' María said as she carefully secured the little statue of the Archangel Miguel inside her shawl.

Nodding, the boy smiled. 'Can you walk for a little bit longer, my dearest ladies?' Still holding each other's hands in a line, the three of them smiled back. 'Yes our dear

Lázaro, I'm afraid we've been sitting down for too long, it's time to walk.' She said as the circle became a line of people holding hands.

'Lorenzo, my friend. As we walk through Ronda, people will come to us. Would you please help them to join the line?' Requested the boy, with a smile as radiant as the dead sun. Lorenzo was ready to do anything in his hand to save the world, so he nodded in acceptance of his new mission. And so, in their atypical formation, the group continued their final journey to save the inhabitants of Ronda.

The boy stopped for the first time shortly after they left. Looking towards an empty corner, near a pile of rubble stained with dry blood, he spoke authoritatively. 'No need to be afraid any longer. We are safe now. Join us, hold our hands and we'll take you to where you should be.'

'Are you taking us to my mother?' A little girl said, as she was carried by a sturdy builder.

'Something like that, little one.' Replied Lázaro with a shadow of sadness, for her mother was dead. 'Come with us, it won't be long until everyone is safe.' He said, with a voice that was impossible to ignore.

'Where are you taking us? She's hurt.' Barked the builder, not very happy about following orders.

'We're going to the Mondragón palace.'

The builder spat bloody phlegm on the floor, cursing the name of the family who had ruled Ronda for all of his life.

'Can you please carry her for a little bit longer? I promise we will be quick.'

'Hm.' The builder grunted, tired, before joining the line. The three ladies looked at the poor little girl with pity in their eyes, but they knew they had to continue moving.

'The palace is not too far. Lord Mondragón needs us for once, we don't want to make him wait. He needs to let time into his cave.' Explained the boy as they returned to their pilgrimage. Lorenzo flinched at the thought of reuniting with his father.

The line of humans navigated the city's ruins, tracing the invisible streets living in their memory. Sorting obstacles was easy, as Lázaro knew exactly where to turn, where to climb, where to stop. Villagers from Ronda appeared from behind every corner; scared, worried and confused.

Lorenzo could relate to them. He helped them walk to the line, where the last person would hold their hands. The fire would be ignited inside their hearts. They all would burn against the End, as bright as the sun before its demise. Even the few animals who remained joined the procession, as hills of destroyed buildings rolled over the plateau.

Only one building could be seen rising above the sea of ruin. The palace still resisted, held by the terrible curse. The closer they got to the Mondragón's hideout, the weaker its beams and pillars started to look. Time slowly requested the seconds, minutes and years that were owed. Lázaro knew that this was the last hurdle, and that the simplest of mistakes would cost everyone's lives, for good. *There's only one way this moment will take us to the future we want,* Lázaro thought as he went through every single branch of the tree of time and possibility.

Arriving at the palace, the company halted. The main entrance was partially covered by the ashes that fell from the sky. The builder and the three ladies commenced to clear it as Lázaro briefed the rest of the villagers. They spread comfortably through the last remains of what used to be a beautiful square. His voice boomed across the place.

'Only me and Lorenzo will enter the palace. It is about to fall apart, so please stay as far away from it as you can. We won't be long.'

'Can we pop our heads in quickly? We've never been invited in, you know? After all these years!' Asked Perpetua, as she finished kicking some of the ashes to one side. The entrance was now clear.

'No one. Please. No one should go in. Everything could change drastically if you did.' Stressed Lázaro with a hint of threat in his voice. The villagers couldn't grasp the extent of the boy's new awareness. And he knew it, so he insisted.

'I promise you that if you stay away from the palace, I will take you to live in it tomorrow.' Smiled the boy, as the three ladies laughed at the ridiculous promise.

'Yes, and I will be the Queen Mother of Ronda!' Mocked Eustaquia, helping everyone who waited in the square to feel lighter amidst so much pain. Lorenzo walked to the boy.

'Are you ready? You know my father is quite stubborn, we may need some help.' Pointed out the traveller.

'He is. All I can feel coming from the inside is oppression and rejection. I cannot see who's inside. And my connection with everything may be lost while we're in.'

'Wouldn't this risk your plan?' Asked an alarmed Lorenzo.

'It could. But if Talita is still there, I need to save her.'

'You're right. Let's go.' The mention of his step-sister convinced Lorenzo, who was eager to be done with the quest.

The two walked in promptly but cautiously, not knowing what to expect from the darkness of the dwelling. The corridors seemed longer than ever. Lázaro used to know the place down to the position of every wooden slab; he could barely recognise it anymore.

The once opulent and shiny interiors were now dull echoes from the past. The curse had taken all of the beauty that they once ostentatiously paraded. All of the curtains were shut, and the wooden vaults had cracked everywhere. The rain of ashes had trickled down its way into the palace, covering everything. The wind, filled with specs of time, moved freely around the rooms, banging doors and pushing the expensive china off their cabinets and tables. The candles had been blown away. The pair entered the room where they last saw the wealthy family praying around a piping hot soup.

The three ladies held their hands tight as they explored the building for the first time. 'If my Leopoldo could see us now. Us! In the Mondragón's!' Said Maria excited.

'Well it's not as nice or beautiful as the rich tongues of Ronda like to spread.' Answered the builder, and before he could spit, Lázaro looked at him. The builder stopped himself.

'What are you all doing here!?' An angry Lázaro exclaimed, trying not to raise his voice.

'I just followed them so they wouldn't get in trouble!' Answered the builder, brushing the guilt off himself.

'This could cost us the end of humanity as we know it! Get out of here, now!' Commanded the boy, as Eustaquia sneakily took a little golden statue of a goat and hid it inside her shawl. The boy pushed them in the direction of the entrance when a deep voice boomed across the room, halting their exits.

'Who is in there? Who dares to break into such an

illustrious place?' The question flew through the air like an arrow aimed at the hearts of the trespassers. The three ladies got so flustered they didn't know what to do, so they ran to hide themselves from the infamous Lord. María and Eustaquia entered one of the rooms where the ceiling had collapsed, falling over a soft pile of ashes. Perpetua covered herself in the shawl and crawled behind the builder, who cracked his knuckles, ready to take down the landlord on behalf of all the workers of Ronda.

Lorenzo raised his hand and whispered, 'Stop whatever you think you are doing. Right now. There's no need to use violence.' Lázaro had turned around and his sole attention laid in the direction from where Lord Mondragon's voice came from.

'Lord Mondragón, it's me, Lázaro. Please would you mind coming out here so we can talk. Ronda needs you.'

'Ronda has never needed the Mondragón, it was the other way round, kid,' the builder muttered.

'If we needed anything, we needed them to leave the town alone!' Perpetua insisted under her breath, loud enough to be heard. Lázaro shushed them in an attempt to keep his plan together. *I am going to have to improvise a little bit if I want everyone to get out alive from this one.*

'I see you have company, Lázaro. Who are my esteemed guests?' Enquired the Lord.

'They are some of the villagers of Ronda, my Lord. This place is not safe anymore. Please take your family and come with us. Before it's too late.'

Lorenzo had moved near the wide french windows where he discovered the creeping End. Signalling Lázaro to be prepared, he drew the curtains with a quick single movement. The dim glow of the end of the world entered the room, hinting at the position of the Mondragón family. The ceiling in the dining room had partially fallen through, and one of the wooden beams had smashed the dinner table right at its centre. The soup tureen had been crushed to bits, and the soup was now spilt all over the floor and the people sitting at the table. Lord Mondragón and his family stood almost in the exact same place where they left them. A tense silence reigned over Ronda. Talita and the lady of the house did not look happy to be retained by the curse. Looking at Lázaro with imploring eyes, lady Mondragón tried to stand up and talk, only to be interrupted by an iron fist that banged what was left of the table.

'Sit down right now, woman! No Mondragón will leave this palace. This is our birthright, you hear me servant boy? So you and your friends can leave right now, or you will have to suffer the consequences.' The eyes of the landlord did not try to hide the fact that he was ready to give up his own life to keep his family under the same roof. Lázaro didn't know what to do, the only thing he knew was that Lord Mondragón had to go with him willingly for the plan to work. Looking around the room he was trying to find something that would help convince the man, and then he saw it. Lorenzo remained next to the window, breathing heavily, ready to tackle his father if necessary.

Looking at Lorenzo, the boy sent a silent message through using the mind language they once shared. *Lorenzo, we have to break down the icy walls of the curse around your father's heart. Forget about violence, only truth and warmth can save this man.* Staring back at him, the traveller heard the words inside his head as clear as if he was standing next to the boy. Nodding, Lorenzo took a deep breath.

Lord Mondragón, who hadn't taken his eyes off Lázaro, was ready to kill.

'Father. Stop, please.' The owners of the palace turned around their heads to face Lorenzo. Lady Mondragón quickly shifted her eyes from Lorenzo to her husband, confused.

'What did you call me?' There was anger in his voice.

'Father. What else should I call the man who loved my mother? Please, end this silly game of yours. Time is back, we need to move on.' Another bang against the table ended up breaking it for good. Talita started sobbing.

'How you dare to come into my house and spurt those venomous claims against me?' The man stood up, dropping his chair in the process, and started to approach Lorenzo, threateningly.

'You banished my mum to Alpandeire, a poor girl, as soon as you heard that she was pregnant. Heartless man.' Lorenzo released emotions that had been brewing for as long as the soup, somewhere in between anger and sadness. The Lord closed his fists ready to break his son's every bone.

'Is that true? Did you beget this man with your sinful lust?'

Lady Mondragón accused, surrounded by an aura even more dangerous than the landlord's. Standing up, she went to Talita and held the girl in her arms. 'How could you do this to me?' She wasn't crying, but filled with steaming anger. Standing next to Lázaro, the boy placed a hand over her shoulder. No fire was ignited, for her own heart had been burning since the beginning of the curse. He was surprised to learn the truth; that she had been affected by the curse as much as he had been - not at all.

'Would you have wanted the whole town to know that I had a lover? Would have you enjoyed your name passed around in whispers around the corners of Ronda? I did it for you-'

'Don't you dare put the blame on me! This is just yours to suffer. This is your sin, this is your lust!' The lady of the house pointed at the man, whose stern appearance had started to crack. 'I was awake all of this time, and I chose to stay by your side! Do you understand what I'm saying? I could have taken Talita and left you! Alone! But I didn't!' Her eyes filled with tears of frustration.

'This is the best quality gossip!'

'A child born out of wedlock!'

'Scandalous!' The three ladies commented as Lázaro flinched.

'This wasn't supposed to happen like this.' The boy said out loud as the builder spat on the floor.

'I paid that woman a lot of money to never tell the boy who his father was. She is the only one who sinned!' The landlord had lost it. Lorenzo pushed him with tears in his eyes.

'Don't you dare talk about my mother like that. She was braver than you'll ever be.' He said, joining Lázaro and his step mother at the other side of the room. The hurt Lord ran towards his son, ready to smash his skull with his bare fists. Everyone in the palace gasped at the attack.

'Lázaro!' They screamed as the fist hit the wrong jaw bone. The boy had placed himself between father and son, and had taken the blow. During the fleeting moment in which their bodies collided, he felt the man's every feeling, and the curse that rooted his heart with darkness. He tried to share his fire with the Lord, in vain. The curse had rotten him to the core. The landlord of Ronda wouldn't survive to see the light of the next day, but Lázaro's embers would allow him to say goodbye with dignity. With his fist still touching the boy's face, the Lord looked at the expressions of horror around him. He knew he had lost.

Lázaro moved the Lord's hand, pushing it down, and smiled at the man.

'I'm so sorry little Lazarillo. I've known you since you were as small as Talita. I didn't mean to hurt you.'

'I know, my Lord. But you know it's time to go, and you cannot come with us. Choose your words wisely as you say goodbye.' Explained Lázaro as everyone started to turn around and walk down the corridor, back to the outside world. The defeated man had lost all the violence within him. He talked to his wife first.

'My soul is tainted by the curse. I won't be going with you all.' He gulped. 'I know there's not much I can say to make things right.' Still holding Talita, his wife teared up. The little girl had fallen asleep, tired from an eternal game of hide and seek. 'I just want to say I'm sorry. And thank you for everything. Please keep Talita safe, and don't let her remember me like this.' He begged his wife, who answered with a quick hug and a kiss on the forehead, before she turned around. She would never see him again, and she was at peace with that.

Only Lorenzo remained in the room.

'And you, my son. I'm sorry for what I did to your mother. She deserved only the best. I was just trying to protect my family. My legacy.' Barely any voice came out from the cursed carcass of the Lord.

'I was your family too, father.' Lorenzo said to a wide eyed man, who was becoming older and more jagged by the second, as time claimed back his rotten soul. 'Goodbye.' his son said as he left the palace. The Lord was left all by himself, being silently judged by the objects with which he would be entombed, and the long shadows they were casting over the carefully crafted wooden walls. A sleeping swallow within the greatest of rooms.

The ceiling started to fall in small pieces, slowly, like a plant that wasn't watered properly. Like a snake losing its scales. As soon as the party left the building, the whole palace joined the ruins of Ronda.

XIII - THE JUMP

In which the end is told; the bells toll for a writer; and Lorenzo receives a song from the future.

Everyone had already joined Lázaro in his last stunt against the End, and still he couldn't find the peace of mind he needed. *Lord Mondragón changed everything, I need a moment to find a path that makes sense. There must be a different way to reach tomorrow.* Struggled the boy, as he manically traversed every single detail of the potential futures ahead of him.

'Lázarillo, can we please stop for a minute. Our knees are cracking as if they hadn't moved in years.' Requested one of the ladies.

'That is because they haven't, my dear Perpetua. Let's sit by those benches around the square.' He pointed at the broken fountain covered in ceramic frogs, who witnessed the procession taking over the resting place. The three old ladies accommodated themselves on the benches dotting the area around the fountain. The other villagers helped the women, making sure their tired bones got some rest before the last leg of their short pilgrimage.

Looking behind him, Lázaro saw the line of villagers welcoming the well earned rest. People from all ages and walks of life had heard Lázaro's call and had followed him blindly, filling their hearts with burning hope.

Lorenzo was starting to feel the wrecking ball of time hitting his body, as exhaustion kicked in after an eternity of endless energy. He had been helping the villagers to walk to the line, pulling them from below pieces of wall and even carrying them whenever the terrain was treacherous. He leaned against one of the orange trees closer to the veranda delimiting the cliffs, and as he leaned against the thin trunk, he found out that the spot had been already taken.

'My guitar! I had completely forgotten I left it here. Silly me.' Excited to be reunited with his instrument, the traveller picked it up and started to tune it, playing around with his lost friend. His mind took him back to the first time he arrived in Ronda, and then to the first time he met Lázaro. *Who could have guessed he was going to save us all.* He turned his head around to face the End; it was so close that the horizon was a massive wall, an approaching tidal wave. He gulped, and started to improvise a little tune to warm up his fingers. The villagers all around the square listened to the traveller's soothing talent, happy to discover music at the end of the world. Lady Mondragón and Talita sat next to him, smiling - the Mondragón knew that when they lost a family member, they had also gained a new one. María left her two friends so she could be closer to the music. It reminded her of better times, of her youth, when her husband would dance with her for whole nights. Leaving the small statue of the Archangel Michael by her side, she sat by the tree next to Lorenzo's, allowing herself to close her eyes and daydream. The orange blossoms above their heads released a luscious scent, silently blessing humanity's last haven of peace. The traveller's fingers seemed to remember every chord, every position of every finger, and he couldn't help but amaze himself at how nimble the guitar felt. *I have missed your sound. You feel so warm and gentle.* Looking distractedly at the statue of the Archangel fighting the serpent, the traveller remembered the winged serpent inside his nightmare. *I should take the guitar with*

me for the rest of the way, just in case it becomes handy.
The whole of the square listened to the man; either crying to the uncertainty laying after a certain end, or smiling to the precious moment of respite they were experiencing, or distractedly remembering the long gone good moments of their lives. Everyone felt grateful for the traveller's music. They didn't know that Lorenzo was getting ready to not run away this time.

Lázaro paced around the square, trying to contain all the information in his head. *There is no available happy ending, but there must be something close enough.* He searched and searched for a way to win, oblivious to the music that Lorenzo was gifting to the remaining people of Ronda. Lifting his head and returning to the last place on Earth, putting aside all of his visions, he focussed his ears on the scene happening in front of him. The people of Ronda felt safe- the strength within their hearts elevating and rejoicing at the guitar's timely melodies. And his eyes opened widely with clarity. Looking at how his friend provided a point of respite before the final fight, a moment of peace, made him discard all of the potential futures he was pondering about.

I have found the closest thing to a happy ending. Thought the boy, as a gut wrenching sadness clawed his guts. At that precise moment Lorenzo looked at him in understanding.

The pair locked their eyes in silence, both knew that it was time to continue walking.

The music stopped.

As the long queue slithered through the ruins of the old town of Ronda, they knew it was about time to cross the bridge. Turning around the corner and walking past the remains of the arched streetway, the destruction gave way to the End. Almost the whole of the forest was completely gone, and the winds rose furious, trying to escape the gaping mouth closing over Ronda. It was clear that the End was meeting itself. Everywhere they looked, the raging black bull advanced, unforgiving. From every single cardinal point, and above them, only darkness. Lorenzo was the first to cross it, turning around midpoint from where he invited everyone to follow by extending his arm.

Everyone followed. The three ladies adjusted their shawls to cover the End from their sight, fervorously praying as their quick steps moved between the old and new sides of Ronda. The builder was the last one to cross it. Pausing at the middle balcony, with teary eyes, he bid goodbye to his family's work of many lifetimes.

'Goodbye beautiful, make sure that it chokes on you when it tries to eat you, ok?' The rough man placed his hand over the carefully carved stone, the same stone that every person he loved had taken care of. 'Yeah, it's been a good ride.' He muttered as he finished crossing it, leaving the sturdy building behind for good. Lorenzo, who was respectfully waiting, comforted the man as they both hurried to catch up with Lázaro and everyone else.

The white bullring shone like a star in the middle of a moonless night; or at least the remaining half of it. A cracked semicircle of whitewashed walls, with tiny square openings all around its halted circumference. Lázaro never understood what was the appeal of bullfighting, but he had never thought twice about it. Only rich people got to actually witness the mindless killing of the animals during the traditional festivities. To him, it was a completely different world that he would never be able to belong to. The drop created when the building split in two was sharp and daunting. *Will we be able to do it?* He wondered as the queue approached the main door of the arena. A figure appeared at the entrance, a woman who waved to the survivors of the world's end.

'Hey, Lázaro! Hurry, my dear!' His mum called. As he realised who she was, he ran with all his might in her direction, forgetting for a minute the power and responsibility he held. He was a child once again.

'Oh mother, how I've missed you!' He ran as they went for the awaited embrace. 'I cannot believe that you are awake. That you're not ill!'

'Well my boy, I wouldn't be here if your friend Lorenzo hadn't saved me from my nightmare. Just like you told me he would.' She explained as Lorenzo walked past them, smiling. He pointed into the building, guiding the villagers inside the arena, as they reunited with all the villagers the boy's mother had already gathered inside. Lázaro's heart had never felt more proud of anyone.

'He truly is our last chance of winning.' He revealed to his mother, whose face turned into stone.

'Is there no other way?'

'Everything will be up to him. It is his choice.'

'I understand, my son.' She reflected on the consequences of Lázaro's words. 'Before we continue I would like you to know-' Her voice was breaking up into a sob. 'I could hear you, every single word, while you were taking care of me. I just want to say thank you. You are the best son I could...' The boy held both her hands in his as they both cried. 'The best I could have ever wished for. I am proud of you and I love you, no matter what.'

'I know mum. I know. I love you too.' Lázaro wiped his tears with his shirt's sleeve as he remembered that he had work to do. 'Thank you so much for bringing everyone into the bullring. That's every single cursed person in Ronda.'

'Not everyone, I couldn't convince that crazy man, no matter what I tried.' She pointed at a building behind the boy, who discovered something he hadn't noticed before. A single wooden desk, solid and dark in colour, stood in the middle of the street. *A random place to get some work done.* He thought, unsure of what he was looking at.

From behind a precarious pile of papers, a funny looking man with a strange beard tried to write on pages that occasionally flew away with the ominous wind. He looked frustrated as he wrote swiftly, crushed the page into a ball and threw it into the growing winds of the end. He repeated these actions, just like a cursed person would have, before time and Lázaro came back.

'I cannot feel him, mother. I doubt he is cursed. He must be something else.'

'What could he be, then?'

'A wit-'

'Don't say a witch, please. I do regret telling you all those scary stories about witches as you were growing up. Not everything and everyone is a witch, my son!' She joked, happy to be reunited with her little one. *He's not little anymore. He's changed.* Worried her mother, as mothers usually do.

Slightly embarrassed, the boy smiled. He reminded himself he no longer was Lázaro alone, he was much more. He left his child persona and focussed on his task at hand.

Everyone breathing should be within the walls of the bullring if we want this plan to work.

'I was actually going to say a ghost. Not a dead one. Since the End appeared on the horizon I have been seeing ghosts from different times. Ghosts from futures that may never take place.' His mother listened attentively. 'They are usually a flash, a mistake. Something that shouldn't be there. This one is different. This one is here.' His words made her hair stand on end. 'I will go and talk to him. Go back inside and prepare everyone.' He commanded with his newly gained voice. Lázaro's mother nodded and disappeared into the bullring, understanding that the orders came from someone other than her child, someone who was many others in just one body.

The man spotted Lázaro. 'You, boy! Bring me another one of this, whatever it is, pronto! I need some more inspiration!'

He is a foreigner, Lázaro judged by the accent. The table was covered with scribbled paper, ink, a fountain pen and empty bottles of liquor. The man was requesting a refill from him.

'Excuse me sir, would you be interested in following me

inside the bullring? Things are about to get ugly out here.' The kid asked politely just as the End roared, closer than ever. The wind whipped their faces and launched a pile of blank paper past the cliffs, straight through the veil. The man, taking his latest page, lifted it and ripped it off once again while grunting.

'It doesn't feel right. It needs to feel right, otherwise I am just wasting everyone's time!' He talked to himself. 'Kid, are you listening? I am so done with this war. Who's winning anyway? And how much of a difference does it even make?' He was drifting with his thoughts, not making any sense. The man flickered, and Lázaro understood.

'What do I need to do for you to return to your time?' Lázaro asked using the voice that carried the authority of the many within him.

'Just get me some more paper, that'll do me for now, kid.' He requested as Lázaro looked around, alarmed at the proximity of the End. The wind came back, this time bringing a cloud of ashes that covered the unwilling time traveller's desk. They shielded their eyes, not being able to see properly around them anymore.

'I really hope you find what you are missing.' The boy muttered, as he started to walk back to the bullring's entrance. A thunderous sound rumbled, coming from the direction of Ronda's old town. The End had claimed the bridge, and was now slowly surrounding the bullring. *Just as I knew it would.* It stampeded through the last few streets and buildings left in Ronda. As it rushed to devour the boy, the evil horizon knocked down a bell tower from one of the churches nearby. The bell tolled as it was swallowed by the ultimate hunger.

'Hey kid!' The time shifter shouted across the deafening final whirlwind. 'For whom are the bells tolling?' Lázaro had too much to worry about, and playing eccentric games was not a priority. 'I think they are tolling for you!' Lázaro shouted back.

In response, a manic laughter filled the air. 'That's exactly what I needed to hear! Thanks, kid!' And by the time that his last word reached the boy's ears, the man, the desk and the papers had disappeared into the shadows. Lázaro entered the bullring and locked the door behind him.

They are waiting.

The broken arena welcomed him into a myriad of expectant eyes. *Mother must have saved at least one hundred souls by herself.* From the inside, everyone had a perfect view of the approaching chaos, which fed the doubts that started to appear inside their hearts. *That's what the End wants.* Lázaro worried, not sure if he'd be able to lead so many people at the same time. The standing half of the bullring was austere; two floors of white pillars and grey arches that used to cover the audience during the hottest days of Summer. Their colour became dull against the albero yellow of the sand covering the ground. Light was almost completely gone from Earth.

'My son,' nudged his mother after seeing his hesitation. 'They are ready to hear what you have to say. Don't think twice about it. You know it's the only way.' She whispered as she hugged him one last time. 'Your father would be proud of you, my dear Lázaro.' The mention of his dad made his heart skip a beat; however, he knew he couldn't afford any emotions. He had to complete the plan. He had to lead humanity into the following day.

Climbing over one of the arched areas where the audience

used to sit, Lázaro took a second to gather his inner voice. Closing his eyes, he felt within himself the authority of his ancestors, and so he spoke.

'This half a circle was originally created to thrive on death, but now, it remains ironically as the last beacon of life. The place where the last group of the cursed ones present a last fight against pure Evil.' He looked around as he spoke, observing the faces of the people of Ronda, hoping that his words were enough to follow his direction. 'Soon, the bullring will become the place where the End meets itself. The End is about to arrive. But we shall not be afraid of it!' The crowd turned to look at Lázaro with respect, for they could tell that the voice coming out from the boy's mouth belonged to the wisest of humans. He rested his eyes on Lorenzo, and a wave of sadness ran through his body. 'What I am about to ask is no easy feat, but you will have to trust me when I say, this is the only chance we have at winning this war. We need to take action, we need to make a decision and follow through with it. We are becoming responsible for our choices and our futures.' Lady Mondragón listened to Lázaro, inspired, while she held Talita even tighter. The three ladies comforted each other, too scared of being too old for whatever the boy was about to ask them to do.

'Listen very carefully, as this is important.' Lázaro continued to provide his final directions to the people of Ronda. 'You will be meeting the End on your own terms. You won't be caught off-guard. You will show the End that humanity created Time, and therefore we are the only ones who can control it.' Lázaro stopped himself before getting too deep into the meaning of what they were about to do. The End got so close that it started to devour the fallen side of the bullring, laying at the bottom of the cliff. *There's no time to waste.*

'You will selflessly give yourself to the End. Form a line near the edge of the cliff, and get ready to jump when I tell you! Quick!'

The crowd broke into anxious chatter, questions and disbelief.

'You said we would survive!' Lady Mondragón shouted from one side of the bullring, as the crowd heckled the boy.

'And you all will, trust me. All we have to do is to jump

into the End instead of letting it destroy us and claim our bodies and souls. I have been past the dark curtain. After the nothingness, there's always something! Please, trust me and do as I say.' The unconvinced humans of Earth continued to chat over Lázaro's instructions, not ready yet to undertake the final sacrifice. *Fear is the way the End wins. A gesture of love towards humanity is the only thing that can save us now.* Lázaro thought. Everything was taking place exactly how he feared it would.

As the End crashed against the remaining walls of the Bullring, the whole place started to shake. Everyone ran around trying to hide, but the End was coming from all directions, and the arches and walls had already started to disappear into the Nothing.

Lázaro looked at Lorenzo. The traveller knew what the boy was about to ask. 'My dearest friend, sorry, but I have to ask.'

'No, my Lázaro. You don't have to.' Lorenzo said as he reached for his guitar. The boy gasped, afraid that there was no hope left for any of the endings he had envisioned 'You were the one who took action before anyone else. You were the one who inspired me. You are the one who saved humanity.' Lázaro said, wondering if that very moment, that very conversation, was destined to happen from the very start of the curse.

Lorenzo nodded and smiled, as he hugged the boy one last time before they confronted the End together. He did not fully understand what was happening. 'I have no clue what to play, but I will try my best.' He muttered, unconvinced, as Lázaro left the embrace. *All of this time I felt I would have a role in this fight. I thought that it would be clear, that it would make sense. How will this guitar save us? Have we lost already?* The traveller thought, as he questioned their last hope. In the sky, his worst nightmare became a reality, the End was meeting itself. Crowns of darkness, looking like horrifying winged snakes, jumped from one side to the other, threading a connecting membrane. Making the End whole. The people of Ronda lost control, and started to scream.

The words of Lázaro repeated inside the traveller's mind. *After the End, there must always be a new beginning. A new sunrise.* In a split of a second, Lorenzo's surroundings shifted and, in the blink of an eye, he disappeared.

'No! Lorenzo!' Shouted the boy as he tried to grab the air where his friend stood up a moment ago.

'What is going on, Lázaro?' His mother asked, trying to calm down the villagers who were losing their sanity.

'I don't know. He's gone...' He looked at her with pure despair in his eyes. 'We've lost.'

The End started to drip; the darkest rain anyone in Ronda had ever seen, slowly tarnishing the people's clothes and souls. Slowly being consumed and digested in the belly of a powerful beast. Everyone panicked as the light went completely off. No one could see anything. Chaos reigned over Earth. A vengeful god laughed upon their throne.

Lázaro kneeled down, powerless, and waited to be smashed by the tyrant who cursed humanity.

Music started to fill the bullring. 'This song is from a future time. A time that starts today. A tomorrow where our story is being told.' Lorenzo's voice presented, as the fire within him raged. His skin started to glow faintly. Everyone in the bullring could see Lorenzo as a lighthouse at the edge of the most treacherous sea. The screaming stopped, as a few timid chords paused briefly the End's final advances. Lorenzo's mouth opened, and a powerful voice came out, resonating within every single person in his presence.

'Hey, hey, hey, the end is near.
On a good day you can see the End from here.
But I won't turn back now, though the way is clear,
I will stay for the remainder.'

Lázaro couldn't believe what he was witnessing. His friend was glowing so bright that the building around them was visible again. Everyone was staring at the traveller in awe, amazed at the white light that covered everything. Lorenzo's light was so powerful and bright that it caught the wooden guitar. Tongues of white fire started to peacefully cover the wooden instrument. The boy couldn't take his eyes off his friend.

'Lázaro, my son. We can see the edge of the cliff. This is our chance!' He woke up from Lorenzo's spell, realising that he had work to do. Standing up once again, he commanded everyone in the crowd.

'If you want to see the sun again, follow me! Grab each other's hands and prepare yourself to jump!' He begged, as people started to do as they were told. Guided by the warmth of Lorenzo's light and the melody of his song, the villagers of Ronda quickly formed a human wall at the edge of the world. Lorenzo continued to sing.

'I saw a life and I called it mine,
I saw it drawn so sweet and fine.
And I had begun to fill in all the lines,
Right down to what we'd name her.'

The End roared in fury, almost trying to drown the song and Lorenzo's living bonfire. Through the noise of oblivion, the crowd could hear the song crystal clear- they weren't listening with their ears, but with their open hearts. They were not individuals, they were all one under the light of a brand new sun. Little white fires lit up over every single one of the villagers's heads like fiery crowns, as they held their hands together. A symbol of unity.

The traveller continued to be consumed by his own power, the flames growing taller and more aggressive against the End's futile attempts at finishing humanity. Lorenzo's blaze burnt through the dark veil over their heads, and where there was darkness, only burning light remained. Talita smiled nervously at Lázaro as he checked one last time that they were ready to jump. The End devoured past the walls of the Bullring, only the sandy surface remained. No one dared to look at the darkness ahead of the cliff, they were focussed on the traveller's song.

'Our nature does not change by will,
in the winter 'round the ruined mill.
The creek is lying flat and still,
It is water though it's frozen.'

'Now! Jump!' Lázaro shouted.

No one moved. The daunting fall was too much for everyone, fear was too real. *I wish I could push them, but they have to go willingly.* Lázaro and his mother looked at each other, not knowing what to do. Suddenly, a ball of spit crossed the air and fell down the cliff, through the End's mist.

The builder looked at his fellow villagers and said. 'It sure takes more than a little jump to scare the citizens of a town on top of a cliff! Let's show this pain in the ass what we're made of!' The young girl he carried laughed at the fact that he had said a bad word, right before they jumped together into the End. Their laughter could be heard even after they disappeared.

After the show of bravery before their eyes, the villagers of Ronda took the final fall. Holding hands, and soothed by the fire within them, they confronted their final challenge. Lázaro sighed in relief. Turning his head around to look at Lorenzo, he cried. *It is working.* The traveller returned his gaze to him, as he shone even brighter. He was surrounded by a ring of fire. Even then, his song continued to provide the needed strength to jump. Most of the villagers had already fallen to their end. Lorenzo's voice filled the air once again.

'So, across the years, and miles, and through,
On a good day you can feel my love for you...'

Lázaro and Lorenzo's hearts were one during that verse.

'My friend.' Lázaro muttered, fully understanding for the first time what he had asked the traveller to do. The remaining line of people kept throwing themselves freely towards the End. It was the turn for the three old ladies; Eustaquia, Perpetua and Maria jumped together as their shawls flew into the wind.

'If our husbands could see us right now!' Wished Perpetua.

'People have been made Saints for less, I'm telling you.' Pointed Eustaquia.

'What would I do without you two! Hahaha.' Shared María, as their laughter joined them in the journey through the mist.

Lady Mondragón and Talita were also ready to make the jump. Looking at her step-son's mastery with the guitar, she felt proud. She promised herself that wherever they went next, she would try her best to create a better future for her daughter. 'See you soon, Lorenzo.' She whispered as she let her body and Talita's drop.

Lorenzo, Lázaro and his mother were the only ones left to jump. Hugging her son one last time, she was ready to leave the Ronda that they knew. The floor started to sink, swallowed by the End, dividing the sandy ground into different floating islands. His mother kissed his cheek and let herself fall backwards, smiling and proud, before it was too late.

The song was about to finish and Lorenzo burnt brighter than ever, delivering the last verse with all the energy he had left. Lázaro couldn't stop looking at him, as his music filled the air and elevated him a few metres over the crumbling arena. The boy knew he had to jump. He knew this was the only way to revert the curse. *Only by a pure sacrifice on behalf of humanity, can we demonstrate that humanity deserves a place in this realm. No matter how many times we're challenged, I know that we will always prevail.*

Lázaro turned around and approached the edge of the world.

I cannot leave him by himself! He turned around once again and looked at the ball of fire that was Lorenzo. Crying, the boy started to run and jump from one diminishing island to the next, trying to get closer to his friend one last time. Like a matchstick which has reached its peak of brightness, the fire that emerged from the guitar framed the travellers body. A surge of menacing white flames stopped the boy in his tracks. Looking back at him, Lorenzo sang the last lines of the borrowed song.

'Will you leave me be so that we can stay true,
to the path that we have chosen?'

Smiling, Lorenzo sent a clear message.

The boy begged, 'Let me stay with you! Please!'

But the song was destined to end, and the fire within Lorenzo was fading away with its last chords. He had no options left. They had to win.

In tears, the boy jumped off the vanishing edge, bathed in the last rays of his friend's light. As soon as the traveller's song finished, Lorenzo was overwhelmed by darkness, and the curse had devoured everything in existence.

The End met itself at the middle of Ronda's Bullring.

The circle completed.

Only Nothing existed.

Reality was no more.

Lázaro led a flock of swallows, through the dark

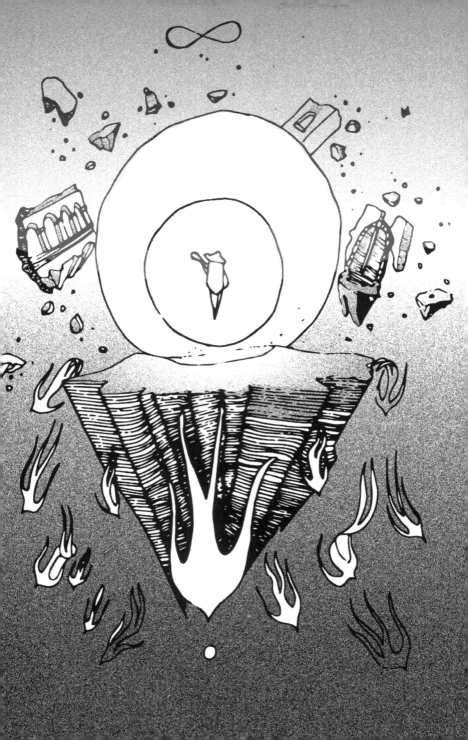

EPILOGUE - THE BEGINNING

And as the night ended, the morning arrived.

A pink horizon blessed the small village of Ronda.
The bread maker woke up early to start preparing the daily orders, the old ladies picked oranges from the trees to prepare sweet cold juice. The bell tolled, as mass was about to start. The fields blossomed under the work of a hundred men, who by sunrise had already been at work for many long hours.

A boy slept in a simple room with a wide open window. His face was covered by a gentle sheet of morning dew, which he appreciated as he slowly woke up to what promised to be a scorching day. That morning was Summer's last one. Lázaro did not sleep too well. He stretched as he walked to the inviting window. He started thinking of all of the stuff he had to do; number one on the to-do list was to go and buy some fruit for his mum and Lady Mondragón, who were busy with the festival's preparations. As he leaned on the window sill, Ronda's cliffs gave way to a land full of life.

On the horizon, in between the new adventuring clouds, a white sun started to travel across the skies; one more day, one more hour, one more minute, one more second.
'Have a good day Lorenzo, please keep us warm, my friend.'
The boy said, before he disappeared from the window and into his house.

And from his newfound perspective, Lorenzo understood: He had stopped being the one who left, to become the one who would always return.

ACKNOWLEDGEMENTS

This book was completed over the six years preceding 2023. Like most of my texts prior to this one, "The End" was born as a present for a friend - a short story to celebrate a connection. Many cakes were baked, much art was produced, and many doors were held open; through grief, discovery, love, and reinvention - if you were there, chances are that part of you is also within these pages.

Thanks to RJ for being patient and reading it all 20 times, to Sarah Higgins for going through the early drafts, to my father for translating those early drafts into Spanish and sharing his love for words with me, and to Conway McDermott for all the stories, especially one about sparrows. Also, thanks to Joanna Newsom for her art and for allowing me to borrow and feature one of her songs (Joanna, if you ever read this, don't sue me, please!).

This book is a Ghibli film; this book is a serene prayer as you fall asleep; this book is a pact with Death, a promise that, after every conclusion, a story always continues.

Gracias a mi familia, a mi madre, por aguantar y proteger mis rarezas.

Y gracias a mi abuela Chati, la loba, por llorar leyendo lo que yo escribía, por creer en mí más que nadie en este mundo..

Carlos Marfil (he/they) is a 35 year old writer from Algeciras, the place where Morocco
and Spain meet, where cultures clash. Liverpool
welcomed him 10 years ago. From this distance,
he explores and dissects their roots and memories: the fine line between tarot, hamsas, ulula-
tion and crucifixes.

The End is his debut novel, a finalist in the
Pulp Fiction 2021 competition. Its first chapter
was published in the award's anthology among
other finalists' chapters.

If you'd like to keep in touch or stay upda-
ted follow Carlos on Instagram @mrmarfil, or
drop him a line at carlos.marfil.r@gmail.com.

Printed in Great Britain
by Amazon